Daniel

Daniel
By Dee Hann-Morrison

ISBN: 9780692369210
LOC #: 12258884681
First published: 2015

Other works by Dee Hann-Morrison

Nazareth
(part I of the Sagan Series)

Elijah
(part II of the Sagan Series)

Lev's Brother
(part III of the Sagan Series)

Solomon's Sons

Even Superwoman Needs to Cry Sometimes

Dedication

******

'Daniel'
is dedicated to the memory
and the spirit of my grandmother,

Mrs. Elizabeth (Pinky) Townsend

Thank you, Ma' Pinky, for the gift of your spirit
that, even on the metaphysical level, continually
nurtures my endeavors
and drives me to greater heights.

Part I---

. . . that from which we cometh

". . . O Daniel, servant of the living God,
is thy God, whom thou servest
continually, able to deliver
thee from the lions?" (Dn. 6: 20)

Chapter 1

"He's gon' kill' her, sho nuf, this time!"Angeline carped. She rung her fingers as she contemplated her younger sister's fate at the hands of a husband who worshipped and adored her, but at the same time, who thought he could beat her into submission and fidelity.

"Yeah. We got to do somethin' . . . quick. All his family's gonna' know after while, and that's gonna be shameful. He's been gone how long, now?" Jessie asked.

Jessie, too, feared for his younger sister's fate, but he feared more in this particular instance, for his oldest sister, and how the unfolding of this particular issue will impact her. He knew that Angeline knew, or *should* know, he surmised quickly to himself, that Josephine's unborn child could very likely have been fathered by her own husband. Jessie mulled over in his mind how one of his sisters had been shameless in her flirtation with men, and none the less shameless about flirting with her own brother in law. Jessie didn't hold Angeline's husband blameless, though. He reminded himself that Tan, on the other hand, had always had a history of womanizing. Throughout their courtship and the early years of their marriage, Tan Francis had earned a reputation for flirting openly with women, even in his wife's presence. There were also rumors that he may have fathered a few children outside of his marriage. With his devoted wife always at home with a house full of children at her knees and no source of income except what Tan provided, Tan had openly cavorted with any variety of women.   Most importantly, Tan knew what marriage--- or being married---meant to Angeline. He, like every member of the Milledge family, was fully aware that being married carried with it a status that Angeline coveted more than life itself.   It was common knowledge that the Milledge's were looked down upon as Bristol Creek low life--- the brood of children with an alcoholic father, who didn't think enough of their mother to marry her until he, himself was dying; the slew of high yellow girls whose dark skinned mother worked at every possible kind of job to keep them fed; the poor family who lived in the run down shack, out of which came yet another illegitimate child just about every year from 1936 – 1944; the family with no moral backbone. . . whose girls were up for the taking to the highest bidder, so to speak.

All of Bristol Creek would have sworn that Gloria Steen's swollen belly in 1935 was the product of having been raped by the drunken old brass ankle who was easily forty years her senior.

"Did the old bat take advantage of that young girl?" towns people questioned.

Still others would comment that ". . .dat child ain't but nineteen or so, and dat dirty old half cracker must be damn near close to a hunnert!"

Anger brewed as the town saw how a trashy old brass ankle mocked a young woman's blackness and left her with child without the decency of making her his wife. And everybody knew that after having cavorted with the likes of the drunken old Milledge man, Gloria Steen had cast herself out of the possibility of respectability ever again. Having borne children for the likes of Jessie Milledge, no decent self respecting Black man would ever touch her. The good folks of Bristol Creek shook their heads in exasperation, lamenting a common southern theme: ". . . dey done gone and mess over and ruint another one a' our womenfolk".

When the young girl kept churning out baby after baby one right behind the other for the next eight years, the people of Bristol Creek shook their heads in even greater consternation. They were embarrassed for Gloria Steen; they were embarrassed for her seven pathetically illegitimate little children; they were embarrassed for the brood of doe-eyed half mulatto children who didn't even know enough to be embarrassed for themselves.

Jessie Milledge, Jr. had a cross to bear in his home town. Not only was he marked with the Milledge label and legacy, but he was burdened even further as his father's namesake. As the carrier of his father's genes and the bearer of his name, Jessie felt that his hometown expected no more from him than what they had seen in his father. They expected the only son of Jessie Milledge, Sr. to carry on his father's tradition of wanton drunkenness and shiftlessness. Jessie, however, was ashamed of his father and all he represented. He felt the needed to

prove that he was anything but is father. As an adult Jessie
had refused to carry the 'Jr.' suffix that his mother had so
proudly attached at the tail end of her only son's name. He
had wished many a day, that his name was not Milledge, at all;
that he could undo all attachments to that heinous legacy of
nothingness. But Jessie loved his mother; loved her more than
life itself, and his mother loved that her children's names were
Milledge. She loved how her children looked--- she loved the
skin color that she knew would give them access to the very
places, things, and opportunities that she, herself, had never
been accorded; she loved the silkiness of the hair that she, as a
child, had coveted. Gloria loved her children and was devoted
to them in every way she knew how, and her children loved
her in return. They were always assured that they had the best
of whatever it was that she could give. Gloria took advantage
of the love she knew her children felt for her. Even at the end
of her life, Gloria Milledge had pleaded with her children to
not let shame run them out of Bristol Creek; she begged them,
especially Jessie, to make good on the Milledge name; to hold
their heads up and proudly forge a path of honor amongst the
very people who had dismissed them as common filth.

Jessie was fully aware that it was only when their mother gave
birth to a boy that their father bothered to marry her. By this
time, though, the elder Jessie Milledge was near death doors
with every kind of alcohol related illness possible. With a
failing liver and dialysis three times a week, 68 year old Jessie
Milledge, Sr. proved to be yet another liability for his
struggling wife and their seven children. By the time Jessie did
the right thing, Gloria Steen (who had had the good sense to
take the mid wife's advice and gave her children their father's
last name) and her seven children were mired in poverty and
steeped in a reputation that rendered them the lowest of the

lowly. They were Bristol Creek trash . . . not the kind of people with whom any self-respecting family wanted any kind of association. They were shunned, openly, and held at arm's length by a community that would only pray for their redemption and pity them in the only way good Christian folks knew how. They were the family with whom parents would never allow their daughters any association, and yet the very family on whom their teenage sons could hone their sexual skills.

While Josephine, Ruby, Sarah, Eva, and Mary seemed oblivious to what Bristol Creek thought of them, Angeline and Jessie --- the eldest and the youngest--- wore on their sleeves the shame that the name Milledge carried. These two of Gloria and Jessie's children were haunted by their family's reputation, and had determined in their hearts, even if not out loud, to correct that image. These two of the Milledge clan had long wanted to be upstanding and respected members of Bristol Creek; they yearned to be embraced as worthy of their community's acceptance. They had vowed to do everything within their power to make right all that was wrong with the Milledge name.

In addition to being aware of what their community thought of them, Angeline and her brother were both also acutely aware of Tan Francis' sentiments about the Milledges, as well. Tan, like the rest of Bristol Creek saw the Milledges as 'less than' himself. He wouldn't have to work as hard to be a good husband, he believed, because he would have been doing Angeline Milledge a favor by marrying her in the first place. With four of Angeline's five sisters having had children out of wedlock, it was a wonder any man in Bristol Creek would do the honorable thing and marry any of those girls, he'd thought.

Tan's proof of their class was further confirmed in the manner in which Josephine Milledge Tracey so blatantly disrespected her own marriage vows.

Tan noticed, even before marrying Angeline, that his intended's youngest sister was not too different than the other Milledge girls. She was what men of Tan's time would call 'loose'.

Ben Tracy's family had openly questioned whether or not Josephine's first child was a Tracey. Josephine's notoriety was that of hanging out at the juke joints, soliciting men to buy her drinks and then paying them with sexual favors. Even if one doubted that Josephine engaged in sexual activity with men other than her husband, her bold and flagrant flirtations by themselves were enough to brand her as a harlot. Those habits didn't stop just because she was betrothed to a young soldier whose family valued education and hard work more than they valued Josephine Milledge's pretty face.

Jessie, like everybody else in Bristol Creek, knew that Ben Tracey had been completely taken in by Josephine's beauty. He was mesmerized by the peach color of her skin; by the lips that were a slight hint of strawberry red; by the eyes a clear hazel with just a tiny hint of blue around the outer rims of the irises; by the perfect arch of her light brown eyebrows. The color of charcoal, himself, Ben was beside himself that he could graze his hands through hair that was silken and the color of wheat. Despite his family's warnings about Josephine Milledge, or what they said about the Milledge clan in general, Benjamin Tracey wanted Josephine by his side; she would make them beautiful children, he'd been known to say. The young soldier had hoped for a house full of children with Josephine's beauty and his focus on achievement; he had believed in his heart of hearts that he could mold his young wife into the lady he believed she was meant to be. As a military man, Ben was assured that exposing his wife to other kinds of life circumstances would help to smooth out her rough edges; would help her settle into her role as wife, mother, and a trophy to propel her husband's career and their lives forward. He had assured himself that all he had to do was dote on her; give her trinkets; give her a home that was better than where she was born. . . all these things, he believed, would make her behaviors as refined as her looks.

Jessie was stunned back into the present by his sister's answer to his question.

". . .'bout seven months or so . . . and here she come up now, four months pregnant!"
Angeline shook her head in both frustration and fear. This, it seems, had been her baby sister's life--- living too close to the edge for comfort; thumping her nose at, and mocking every opportunity to bring some semblance of grace or honor to the Milledge family; thumping her nose at, and mocking every opportunity to bring some grace and honor to her own life.

"So, by the time he comes back state side his wife will have a two-month old infant . . ." Jessie contemplated quietly, then added, ". . . yeah, even as dumb as he is, he can figure this one out".
Jessie exhaled an exasperated breath as he raked his right hand through the fine light brown hair that had, even the age of 28, already started to thin and turn gray at the temples.

"She come to my house a-hoop'in an' holler'in . . . talk'in bout Ben gon' kill her this time . . . ask'in me to help her. I can't help her get rid'a this one; this one too far gone!" Angeline declared, still wracked with concern for her sister's safety.

"Well, Angeline, you 'bout right on this one. She done mess up now. He gon' beat the daylights outta' her this time".

"Jessie, he gon' kill 'er. She done shame Ben so much, even his own family shame for him" Angeline said, fanning her face with her hand.

Jessie looked at his sister's face intently. He could see the worry lines around her eyes and her mouth. He could see the age on her face that was probably put there by a lifetime of anguish. Jessie easily saw the late forties, maybe even early fifties on a face that should have been flaunting the radiance of the mid thirties. He shook his head, and while Angeline assumed her brother's annoyance was prompted by Josephine's untimely pregnancy, she was wrong. Jessie's irritation had more to do with Angeline. His assessment of his eldest sister's woes centered around what her life had been like and how, despite her marriage to the military, he believed she was probably no better off in marriage than if she were single. In his estimation her burdens may have increased exponentially in being married to Tan Francis.

In addition to having six children to take care of, Angeline had her husband to worry about, as well her sisters. As an adult Angeline had still fancied herself her siblings' parents; she had continued her tradition of bailing adults out of situations that were of their own making . . . of their own doings; situations, he reminded himself, silently, that were borne of his other siblings' blatant immaturity and disrespect for personal responsibility. Jessie looked into his sister's eyes that even at the age of thirty –five, had already had the fading discoloration of age, and all at once he was consumed by a pall of sadness. He remembered thinking to himself "... its so unfair... she has so little enjoyment in life ... even now ...".

Even as the youngest child, Jessie knew that Angeline Milledge Francis had never been a child. From the time she was knee high to a grasshopper she was busy taking care of people or things. No more than seven years old and Angeline Milledge knew how to stand in the food stamp line for her mother; she was practiced in convincing Duke Power Company to let them have electricity for just a few more days '... until Mama can come down there and pay y'all'; she knew to get her sisters and brother out of bed, fed, and dressed for school. With five sisters and a brother to rear while her mother scrubbed floors and cleaned chamber pots for Bristol Creek's wealthy and almost wealthy, Angeline had a world of worries even before she was seven years old. By the time her daddy came to reside in the run down shack they called home, an eight year old woman was cooking meals, washing clothes and hanging them out to dry on the old wire clothes line. When old man Jessie made his home with his children the only thing he brought with him was more work for Angeline. Now she had to nurse his frail and ailing body along with her other chores. When here daddy moved into their modest and already inadequate home, Angeline was not even nine years old, and had assumed the roles of mother, maid, and now, nurse. On top of all her other duties, she was now charged with dispensing medications, feeding, and emptying the chamber pot for a hateful old man who constantly barked orders and complained about how they were carried out.

Angeline had always wanted so much more for the Milledge family; she wanted them to be respected members of the Bristol

Creek community; she wanted them to not have to carry the burden of their father's drinking; she wanted them to not have to wear their own illegitimacy on their faces; she wanted them to not carry the shame of poverty on their shoulders. And, she made it her duty, even in childhood, to ease these burdens for the six that came after her.

"Does she even know who the daddy is?" Jessie ventured the question with caution. He looked piercingly into his sister's light brown eyes; eyes that were cloudy with age long before they should be; eyes that looked like they belonged to a 60-year old instead of to a 35 year old. Jessie searched for truth; he searched for what he believed his sister knew but would never tell. In her usual fashion, she had again become a wall behind which yet another person could hide: her husband, this time. Angeline quickly averted her brother's gaze. She shrugged, then continued with her rant.

"I don't know, and it don't too much matter, Jessie! We all know how Ben beats her behind; she always marked up and bruised up. The last time he dang near beat her to her death. You would think that would teach her a lesson . . . to stop runn'in around so! . . . and God knows the man give her everything she want . . . she don't want for noth'in! All he want from her is to stop sham'in him so; stop mak'in a fool of him and a mockery of they marriage. All she got to do is sit her behind home, clean the house, and take care a' that one child. Is that too much to ask? It's like its somethin' wrong with her . . . like she can't help herself. And now this! She done gone too far . . ." Angeline shrugged and added, ". . . I don't know what to do. You know as well as I know he gon' kill her dead!"

"Who else knows?" Jessie asked, thoughtfully.

"God only knows, Jessie. I would bet you she done talked to Ruby, though. You know they close and God knows they cut from the same old rancid cloth" Angeline continued her lament, as she shook her head from left to right in despair.
"Lord, Jesus! That's all we need. If Ruby knows, we can say the whole world knows" Jessie said.
"She didn't tell me that she told Ruby, but you know, sho' as you born, that if she come to me with this mess, she done been to one a' them. They don't come to me 'til they done try everything else. I'm the last one they come to . . . when they done made a mess of they life, then they come to me . . . like I'm supposed to save them".

Jessie smiled to himself as he listened to his sister go on about being the family hero. He knew that, in truth, it had become Angeline's mission in life to save her sisters. He was too well aware that it wasn't always that his other sisters ran to Angeline, but rather that it was usually Angeline who couldn't resist any opportunity to don the hero's cape. Now he shook his head as he considered the pathology in what his sister would like to present as altruism. He, like every member of his family, his in-laws included, knew all too well that as long as Angeline could busy herself in everybody else's crisis, then she didn't have to deal with the sham that she called her own marriage; as long as Angeline was busy putting out fires in Ruby's or Sarah's or Josephine's backyard, then she didn't have to deal with the inferno in her own household. Jessie's brows furrowed as he thought more in-depth of how the eldest had come to use the handy excuse of everybody in the family needing her help to manage their affairs as the perfect smoke screen for not dealing with her own philandering husband.

Jessie was fully aware that if he wasn't careful, Angeline would be trying to save him too; she would be none too happy, he smiled to himself, to run his household as if it were her own. Jessie learned early in his marriage that he had to feed his oldest sister with the proverbial long handled spoon. His wife had warned him early on in their relationship of Angeline's propensity to cross the lines into their business, and she had uttered a stern warning about those kinds of boundaries. He recalled his' and Frances' discussion on this topic even before their wedding and remembered how his then father-in-law to-be capped that talk with one of his own. Jessie was amazed at how obvious his sister's behaviors had been to everyone but himself. He had come to understand in time that he simply didn't want to see his sister in the light that was blaringly obvious to Frances Goode and her family. He didn't want to believe that there was malice in his sister. ". . . after all. . ." he reasoned, ". . . she is my sister".

It wasn't until Jessie had had the opportunity to speak with Rev. Goode about the issue that he had come to realize that Angeline's constant meddling wasn't malice at all. Rather, he learned from a man he considered to be wise, it was just how his family had grown up protecting one another. Jessie reminded himself of Rev. Goode's exact words: ". . .and with Angeline having been the "Protector In Chief" it was just difficult for her to relinquish that role". Rev. Goode had explained further, that with Angeline's own marital issues threatening to disintegrate that illusion she had created, and not wanting to deal with those, it just made sense that Angeline would, if the opportunity availed itself, absorb herself in the distraction of other people's lives. At the end of their pre-marital counseling, though, Jessie had gotten clarity on what was happening. Rev. Goode had reminded Jessie in a clear and stern tone that his responsibility was to cleave unto the woman whom God had ordained as his wife. It was from that biblical lesson that Jessie was thoroughly assured and perfectly committed that he would never allow Angeline access to any discord in his own marriage. He had committed also that he would not, under any circumstance, engage Angeline in any discussion of her husband's philandering.

At once Jessie's roaming thoughts returned to his sister's kitchen and to her anguished pleas for help in saving their youngest sister from an already angry and exhausted husband. Because he really wasn't listening to Angeline, his best response was to pose to her yet another question.

"What did she say when she came to you, Angeline?" Jessie asked, his question laden with both frustration and fear.

"I told you, Jessie! She come to my house cry'in; telling me Ben gon' kill her!" Angeline yelled, as if her brother hadn't heard what she was saying all along.

"Okay . . ." Jessie said soothingly, taking his sister's hands into his own and stroking them comfortingly, then added ". . . don't get your blood pressure up over this. We'll figure somethin' out". As if an after thought, Jessie's eyes stretched, ". . . she hasn't been out there in the streets, has she? I mean, parading around Ben's family, has she?"

"God, I hope not. You know they can't stand her as it is . . . they never thought she was good enough for Ben in the first place . . . and she just keep prov'in 'em right . . . over and over . . ." Angeline's voice trailed off, as she shook her head from side to side.

"You say four months . . . is she showing?" Jessie asked.

"You know she don't hardly show 'cause she so thick in the hips. . . she carry Benjy in her hips, for sure. But by the eighth or ninth month it's gon' be hard not to know . . . and when the baby get here, how she gon' hide that? . . . its gon' be impossible not to know" Angeline declared with an air of sarcasm lacing her last words.

"So, we runn'in out 'a time to figure somethin' out, then" Jessie contemplated.

Chapter 2

"We can all sit 'round here like we so high and mighty . . . like we better'n everybody else, but we all know the truth" Ruby declared with a sneer at her eldest sister.

"What you go'in on about now, Ruby?" Sarah asked in feigned innocence.

"You know. . ." Ruby sniffed, arching her neck so that her narrow nose pointed towards the ceiling, then added, " . . . we all know. . . all a' us sitt'in round this table know".

Angeline Francis sat quietly. She had a good idea what her sister was getting at, but had decided before hand that today was not the day to get into yet another fight with her sisters . . . any of them. As the eldest she had assumed the charge of taking care of them, even in adulthood. Angeline prided herself on her lifestyle. She was the consummate wife and mother; she was the representative of middle class-ness. She had presumed that her life would serve as an example that all her siblings would want to follow; *should* follow. Angeline had decided with Jessie before this meeting that despite whatever punches Ruby, Sarah, or Eva tossed at her, she was not going to sink to their level . . . not today, anyway. Plus, she was too exhausted to fight. With taking care of six children and always wary of her husband's wandering eyes and wandering hands, Angeline found that she was running out of energy. With her sisters' knowledge of her husband's cavorting, she knew, further, that she didn't have much of a leg to stand on when her family punched holes in her marriage.

Angeline looked to Jessie for strength and guidance for how to respond to the fire Ruby and Sarah were stoking.

Jessie was not surprised that he could assemble all his siblings within a short period of time. None of the Milledge women worked except Mary. They were all housewives or living off the mercy of taxpayers. This fact assured Jessie of their availability for a daytime meeting. So within a week of learning of Josephine's ill-timed pregnancy, all the Milledge children had agreed to meet to figure out the best course of action.

Jessie also didn't want his own wife to know what was going on with his family, so he had pretended to be at work, himself. In the eight years of their own marriage he had taken a good bit of ribbing from the Goode family. He had had to prove himself a hundred times over to Rev. and Mrs. Goode before they would bless their daughter's union to a Milledge. Even though he and Frances were happily married with their own family, Jessie always felt like, as a Milledge, he continued to be under the microscope; he felt like proving his worth as a decent

human being was a never-ending task. His family's history---
his father as a drunkard and a brass ankle and his mother as
the women who boldly bore children out of wedlock---would
keep him marked as questionable in character. Despite his
extra efforts to afford his family not just the necessities of life,
but a few of the luxuries as well, Jessie always felt like he
merely hovered on the periphery of the Goode family---an
interminably contaminated interloper still trying to gain
admission to that which is clean and righteous. When scandals
like this occurred, Jessie worked hard to keep them out of
earshot of his in-laws, as if his sisters' slanderous behaviors
would be a direct reflection of his own moral disposition.

As the family patriarch, and having little faith in either of his
sisters' spouses (meaning husbands and/or boyfriends) to be
discreet about Josephine's situation Jessie, again, assumed the
alpha position and advised his sisters they should meet on this
Tuesday morning at 11:00 AM at Angeline and Tan's house.
The time of day, of course, would assure that Tan would not be
present.

Josephine sat to the right of her brother, who had assumed a
seat at the head of the table in the Francis household. Jessie
had assumed this position as if he, indeed was the head of his
sister's household.
Despite the tensions that existed between the sisters and their
propensity for fighting, Jessie was assured that they could and
would all come together to save their baby sister's marriage
and possibly her life. He recalled that as children it had always
been the Milledges against the world . . . or, at the very least,
the Milledges against Bristol Creek, South Carolina. They had
fought many a battle, he recalled, and they had been victorious

primarily because of the lessons they had learned early in life: that they had to stick together; that they were all they had. So, while the situation before them was tenuous at best, even Jessie believed that they could and would somehow work together to cover up this shame.

"aaaahem. . . ." Jessie declared order by clearing his throat.
Ruby looked at her watch and exhaled impatiently.
Sarah spoke up rather bluntly and without the benefit of a prelude: "We all know why we here; no need to dress noth'in up. Josephine in trouble and Ben gon' kill her behind when he get back from wherever they done send him this time".
Jessie exhaled a quick puff of air. In his position as chair and chief family problem solver, this was not the way he had planned for this to go. In all honesty, though, he was not shocked that their meeting was headed in this direction. "This . . .", Jessie acknowledged to himself, ". . . was par for the course; this is all we know---how to shout and point fingers at one another". As he sat in silence waiting for Ruby and Sarah to flush out their systems of long standing resentments against Angeline and Josephine, he was reminded of how incredibly different his wife's family was from his own. He thought about how the Goodes exuded civility and class; how they spoke cordially and respectfully to one another, even when what they had to say was critical. He thought about how his father-in-law presided over family gatherings and how all members of the family accorded him unyielding respect. Jessie's attention was brought back to his sister's dining room by the increasing volume of snickering, accusations, and general discord.
Sarah's declaration of her baby sister's fate caused Josephine to erupt in a fit of convulsive sobs. Angeline and Eva rose from

their seats to comfort their distraught baby sister. Josephine's weeping seemed to increase in volume and intensity in direct proportion to her next to the eldest sister's anger. The red that slowly crept up Ruby's neck was now consuming her face and even her eyes. Ruby's pupils became as sharp as pinpoints and her breathing became shallow with rage.   As if she could no longer sit with what she was feeling, Ruby rose from the chair with the thick plastic covered seat cushion. She started a slow pace around Angeline's pristine and elegantly furnished formal dining room, with her arms akimbo, at first.   As she spoke her pace picked up in proportion to the octave of her speech and the movements of her arms.   Although Ruby made no mention of the décor of his sister's dining room she couldn't help but notice the extravagant and ornate china cabinet filled with trinkets to memorialize her sister and her husband's travels courtesy of the Unites States Army.   A life, she noted to herself, far removed from her own and from that of Sarah and Eva; a life reserved, Ruby noted, only for two of the Milledge sisters--- Angeline and Josephine.   Ruby couldn't help but be reminded of how different Angeline and Josephine's lives were from those of people like herself and two of her other sisters; people who lived, she made a mental note, in public housing and who squeezed their dozen or so children into three tiny bedrooms of lead-painted concrete walls; a life where there were no dining rooms or china cabinets; a life not too far removed from the one in which they had all been born; in which they all grew up; and in which, according to Ruby's estimation, they all had survived.

Every item in the huge dining room that met Ruby's almost hazel colored eyes served the purpose of compounding the resentment she felt towards her eldest sister.   As she looked at the various portraits of the perfect American family---devoted wife, and six adorable and well dressed children, all smiling as they surround the uniformed and decorated soldier---she became more and more angry. She was angry for what the Francis family had compared to what she didn't have; but she was more angry for what they perpetrated that she knew wasn't true. Ruby knew that the picture was a farce; she knew that her sister's smile was pasted on for the purpose of the camera and that it couldn't have come from the place where true smiles are born; she knew that the smile Angeline wore did not come from her heart. Ruby looked at the glazed look of pretense in each of her nieces photographed eyes as they smiled for the camera; she knew that her brother-in-law had fathered more children than the six seen in that family portrait. She was angry that her brother-in-law came to call at her house when she wasn't at home and that she'd had to keep him away from her young daughters. She suspected that he had very probably been touching his own daughters inappropriately, as well. Ruby was incensed that her nieces in the picture had snubbed their first cousins as being ghetto children; she resented that Angeline would not allow her precious middle class children to visit any of the Milledge family members except for Jessie and what she would easily describe as his pretentious children. All these, and a million other little sparks of buried resentments met at an unlikely place in her throat and ignited words that spewed out of Ruby like venom.

"Why don't you tell 'em, Jo . . . tell 'em who is responsible; tell 'em who knock you up!"
Ruby's request came out more like a challenge . . . a dare . . . maybe even an order; an order that would serve as the equalizer; an order that would demonstrate to Angeline that every person around that table knew her life, and particularly

her marriage, wasn't as perfect as the family portrait on the wall suggested.

At Ruby's demand that Josephine reveal the name of her baby's father, the room fogged over in silence. With unspoken words hanging in mid air, every single one of Gloria Milledge's seven children froze in sudden quietness. The silence was so thick it was tangible; it hung like a thick black curtain daring to be pushed open.

"Ruby, I don't know if that matters at this point", Jessie offered calmly.

"The hell it don't!" Ruby spewed.

When the room, for the second time within a matter of just a few minutes, went into another dead silence, Mary spoke up.

Mary was the Milledge sister who was smack in the middle, chronologically, and politically. Mary was the fourth of Gloria and Jessie's seven children, and the Milledge child who listened attentively to both sides of family disputes. She was the sibling who weighed in only as a means of resolving the issue. While the Milledge daughters learned early in life to defer to their only brother, precisely because of his maleness, they had all come to take stock in Mary's opinion, as well. Even at the age of thirty-one Mary was the member of the Milledge clan who seemed to have been endowed with both wisdom and calm. She was never out to prove or disprove her family's worth or value, neither in Bristol Creek nor anywhere else, for that matter. Mary Milledge had learned to embrace the world on her own terms and to deal with life as it was given to her, and was likely the least emotionally expressive of a family inordinately prone to emotional outburst; a family that fought to the bitter end; a family that was at once warm and welcoming and at the same time closed and clannish.

"It *does* matter, Jessie. It matters indeed. In this case it matters more than anything who the other responsible party is" Mary declared quietly, but unapologetically.

"Josephine is a grown woman" Jessie insisted.

"Yes she is, but she *is* a woman . . . and that baby she's carrying has a mother and a father!" Mary said without flinching or cowering to her brother's unspoken authority.

Although Josephine was still sobbing almost inconsolably, she was now being comforted by Ruby, Sarah, and Eva. Angeline had resumed her seat next to Jessie at the table. She looked around at members of her family knowingly.

" . . . and since Josephine is going to have to suffer as a result of this, I think the father of this child should also assume some responsibility" Mary declared, directly and succinctly.

Mary's words to the assembly of Milledges were uttered as if they were a statement of fact rather than as a reflection of emotion. Her eyes travelled around the entire table, making a stop to look piercingly into the eyes of each of her siblings in their own time. After her own brand of silent demand for reason in managing what was before them, Mary added, " . . . she's beyond the point of terminating the pregnancy, so there *is* going to be a baby. That's a given! . . . and that baby she's carrying *is* a Milledge. That child has our blood coursing through its veins. None of us can judge how it got there or how it will get here, but we all know that it exists and so it is our responsibility to help take care of it. We certainly can't let Ben Tracey come back here and . . . well . . ."

"Hell, he'll not only kill Josephine, he'll kill the child, too!" Eva's sudden words were offered in a panic, as if this thought had come to her as an epiphany just in that very second.

"So, what are ya'll say'in?" Sarah asked?

Chapter 3

The fat baby with his pudgy little angelic baby face and his pink flushed lips, squinted his eyes as he looked around at his new home. He was just about the cutest thing his big sisters had ever seen. He reminded them of pictures in their Sunday school books of cherubs.

". . .heaven-sent. . ." they thought, and he would come to be precisely that for at least five little girls whose gender had been a gross disappointment to their father. Tan Francis, a man who had historically demonstrated blatant disrespect for the opposite gender, had tolerated the fact that his wife had given him a girl as their first child. He would forgive her for this, he'd thought, but he became increasingly relentless in his pursuit of a male child. As if the gender of their children were the purview of his wife, Tan had become close to abusive every time the nurses announced that the new addition to their family had been yet " . . . another girl". His daughters, too, had come to hope for a brother as if having one would be, in and of itself, some kind of special blessing. Every child after Angela was a disappointment and each one was well aware that she was. In turn each child had prayed that the next would be a boy. So, on that August morning when Angela and Tan brought home a bundle wrapped in blue, every child in the house rejoiced.

"Like a doll come to life" Jessica chirped as she tickled the soft soles of her new little brother's plump feet.

Angeline's effort at feigning post-partum fatigue was not too far removed from what she was really feeling. She was exhausted all right. Although she had not given birth, she was in pain and thoroughly tired of this game she had engaged in with her family---with her sisters and brothers, mainly. As she thought about their little arrangement for Daniel, she had second and even third thoughts. She wondered now, four months after that fateful meeting around her own dining room table, whether this had been a good decision; whether this was something she could do; whether this plan was a viable one. She remembered all their faces---their unspoken words; their silent taunts at her life; their quiet assertions about this baby's father. She also wondered about the challenges she would have to face in asserting her authority within her own family that she was Daniel's mother---Daniel's *only* mother. Angeline never had the formal education that Mary had, but she knew even before Mary told her so that ". . . once this deed was done. . ." she would have to keep her distance from her sisters and possibly her brother, too. Angeline uttered a private grunt as she looked down at the eight-pound child swaddled in her arms.

"Who would ever doubt?" she asked herself. "He looks just like my children . . . all six of 'em are marked; they got that Francis mouth and them awful bulging Francis eyes . . . and this one's got'em, too".

Angeline watched with a mixture of pride and resentment as her young daughters fawned over their new baby brother. She watched as her husband smiled proudly at his son; his first son; his only son. Even as she thought this, Angeline had to admit that she couldn't be sure of that either.

". . .was this Tan's only son? . . . was this his first son?" she asked silently?

She placed the infant in the white bassinette next to her bed and watched as the baby lay, wrapped up in its blue and white hospital issued blanket, kicking and screaming for something---food, maybe, or a diaper change. She looked at her husband with an eye that clearly suggested that he had better get up out of bed and tend to his child. Tan, however, looked back at his wife with the facial message that spoke loudly and clearly 'this is *your* family secret . . . you'd better start acting like a loving and devoted mother . . .'. Angeline heard the unspoken threat, and immediately resorted to her position as family savior. Now, in addition to saving her sister from her husband's wrath, her bigger charge was saving this child. She knew she had to save him from the shame of his conception; the shame of his birth; and the secret which every member of his family knew, but which he must never know. Angeline knew that she couldn't control her sisters' tongues, and she suspected that although they had all vowed to never reveal the plan they had concocted back in April, they could be unpredictable; they could fall prey to what they believe was love and share the secret with whomever was their current lover; she knew this would be the mantle they would hold over her head forever and that they could, and would, retaliate in anger. As she, probably for the first time, considered the breadth of the contract for secrecy into which she had just inadvertently entered with her sisters, she shuddered in fear. It was at this moment that Angeline realized that in having taken part in this fiasco she had just as good as sold her soul to her bitter and resentful sisters. She had given over her life to three women - - -Sarah, Ruby, and Eva--- in particular, that could control her with this secret for the rest of her life. As she lay in bed she realized that she had to make some sweeping changes in order to protect this baby . . . her baby . . . her son, as well as to protect her other children. Angeline was assured that there was only one of her siblings that she could count on to never reveal the secret---that was Mary. All the others, she realized, could and very probably would, concede to their spouses the details of Daniel's conception and birth; of his very existence. This idea nagged at her profoundly, and she found herself looking at her son with loving motherly eyes. . . with her sole ambition being one of protecting this precious child who was the product of sin.

As she lay in her fabricated postpartum bed, Angeline's six daughters catered to her every need. Even the four-year old twins pitched in. They were giddy with the excitement of having a new baby in the house. Even more, they were infected with their father's contagious excitement over having a son, at last. Daniel had become the family's little prize all wrapped in blue. Angeline, herself, was starting to feel the glee, but wasn't sure if she could afford to allow herself that kind of pleasure. Her mind raced in a million directions as she looked at the child who resembled her husband even more than the six that she was absolutely certain he had fathered.

During her postpartum convalescence, Angeline replayed the tape in her mind at least a thousand times---her sisters 'almost' accusations; her husband's easy acceptance of the notion of them covering for Josephine. She considered that neither she nor her husband of thirteen years had typically made rash decisions. They had been deliberate in all their choices, carefully discussing options and weighing pro's and con's so as to maximize the benefit they would or could reap from their decisions. The one thing she knew about Tan with absolute certainty, was that he would never participate in such a scam if he was not, in some shape or form, a beneficiary. Tan had, on more than one occasion, voiced his disapproval of Josephine's scandalous behaviors. He had often commented on how shamefully flirtatious she could be. And although Tan had never raised a hand against his wife, he often insisted that he understood why it was that Ben Tracey beat his wife all the time. What he didn't understand, he often told Angeline, was why Ben just didn't " . . . leave that whor'in woman". Although Angeline remembered feeling the cold slap of an insult when she first heard her husband describe her youngest sister in such harsh terms, over the course of nearly a decade and a half, she had become hardened to his ugliness when it came to Josephine.

Angeline recalled, in her convalescing place, that her husband was even more sensitive about his sister-in-law's tawdriness because Ben, like himself, was a service man. Tan and Ben seemed to have bonded on that common note. Unlike Ruby's, Sarah's, or Eva's husbands and boyfriends, who had amounted to nothing, Tan Francis and Ben Tracey had deemed themselves and their families to be light years above those of the other Milledge sisters. They all respected Mary, however, questioned her sexuality since she had poured herself into her education and career.

"He didn't argue; he didn't put up the fight I was prepared for" she thought to herself.

Angeline had prepared for war when she had agreed to ask her husband to go along with her family's ploy to save Josephine from certain death. She had expected her husband to raise hell and everything above it in his protestations.   When she carefully broached the subject she was blown away when Tan said, 'okay', as casually as he would if she'd asked him to pass her a stick of gum.

"We knew this was gon' happen someday . . . so, yeah we'll just take the baby. What's one more to feed. . ." Tan had said and rolled over to go to sleep.

Angeline remembered sitting up in their bed in awe. She wondered, ". . . did he just say yes, or was I dreaming?"

She even remembered that she didn't even have to confirm that they had had the conversation, as Tan himself, did this the very next morning as she stirred the huge pot of oatmeal. "Remember to get whatever paperwork we need to make this thing legal, okay. I don't want no mess from none a' yo people".

Angeline had taken Daniel out of the bassinet. She looked down at him all snug in the crook of her left arm. He sucked on the bottle like his life depended on it. As he gobbled down the Similac he occasionally looked up at her with pleading eyes. His one-week old head wobbled from left to right on his rubbery neck as she propped him onto her left shoulder to burp.

The inevitable nagged at her. She wondered if she was really going to be able to do this; was she going to be able to love this child like her own? Was she going to be able to look at this child for the rest of her life and know . . . but pretend like she didn't know? Was she going to be able to nurture him like she nurtured her six daughters? Was she going to be able to not hold him accountable for his mother's . . . and his father's actions? Was she going to be able to not be angry at this child because his mother mocked all that was important to her?

"Could I dare . . . should I dare . . . love this little person? Was there more I should have asked before I took this on? . . . What pieces of this puzzle had I not considered in taking on this kind of responsibility? Would this come back to haunt me later? Would this innocent baby be haunted by what he didn't know?" These were only a few of thousands of questions that kept rushing to the forefront of Angeline's mind, yet even as these questions pounded at her head for an answer, she knew it was too late; she couldn't throw this fish back into the water.

For less than a split second Angeline entertained the notion that Josephine might have a change of heart; that she might come wanting her baby back, but just as quickly as that thought emerged, she was able to quash it. Angeline counted on the fact that Josephine was too smart to compromise her life or her livelihood . . . not even for this baby. Angeline had to come to terms with what was really eating at her: how was she going to deal with her family . . . her sisters.

"That damn Ruby and Sarah. . ." Angeline said under her breath, ". . .they know. They know and they'll hold it over me for the rest of my life. They know who this baby belong to; they know 'xactly who the daddy of this child is . . . and that's the weapon they'll use to keep me in my place from now on".

Angeline asked herself all these questions as she contemplated what had been done. And on cue, as if he, himself was appointed to answer his new mother's unspoken questions, the child expelled the gas that had settled on his little chest in a smooth and clean release of air. Angeline took Daniel down from her shoulder and inspected his tiny infant face for the hundredth time in the last forty-eight hours. She wasn't sure what she was looking for. The baby looked back at her with something of a knowing in his own light brown eyes. The eyes buried behind the wrinkled skin of a newborn's lids spoke a truth louder than any spoken word. In that instant something happened; in that nanosecond when the glint of Daniel's infant eyes caught that of Angeline's in just the right way, something profound happened; at that second a truth became known . . . a truth that existed only between a mother and her son. The only question that remained after that visual encounter was whether Angeline would one day tell Daniel; or whether Daniel would one day tell her.

Chapter 4

Tan had prayed for God's forgiveness, and in looking at the squalling child in his wife's arms, he somehow felt like his request had been granted. On top of that, he told himself, God had granted him his greatest wish: a son; a boy to carry on a name that he, himself, couldn't own as his own; a male child to right what was desperately wrong with his very existence.

"Someone . . ." he said silently, ". . . to bring honor to a name that reeked of the rancid stench of shame". Long before that moment, Tan had given up hope of himself bringing honor to the Francis name. God knows he had hopes of doing that, but as he looked at this child, his only hope was that his namesake would be so much better than he, himself, or his own father before him. Tan thought of his own harsh upbringing and swore again, as he had done at least a hundred times throughout his forty two years, that no child of his would ever grow up like him; no child of his would ever have to face the shame of poverty; no child of his would ever have to hide his face behind namelessness . . . to live with the stigma of being a bastard.

Tan had never known his father. He never even had a name for the man whose blood he had coursing through his veins. The child of an unmarried woman whose own morals were put in question by her out-of-wedlock pregnancy in 1929, he had been sentenced to a lifetime of scorn and derision. The disgrace of knowing that he had never been worthy of his father's acknowledgement had haunted him for all his days.   There were times ---lots of time---he had wondered whose son he was. There were times that he'd dared to compare some of his own physical features with men in their local community, hoping to connect himself to someone or something; hoping to connect himself to a name or a face, if nothing else. To ask about his paternity would have been daring and disrespectful, so instead, he spent a lifetime speculating about who his father was. He had heard rumors and had listened to his mother's family cast innuendos, but no man had ever stepped forward to own him; to legitimize him; to rescue him from the heavy burden illegitimacy had cast upon his childhood shoulders.

And yet, he was reminded, as he looked into his tiny son's light brown eyes, that to this place he had come . . . here he stood. . . dangerously close to all he had spent a lifetime running away from.

"Yeah, this is definitely God's work" Tan rationalized in silence. This line of reasoning had been Tan's salvation; the crutch on which he would lean when his behaviors had been simply outside the bounds of adult reasoning. He had mustered every ounce of common sense to explain to himself how he had gotten to this place, and when logic was scarce, he had pulled out what had always been his trump card: 'the working of the Lord'. Tan looked at the boy child who his wife and daughters seemed to adore and came to embrace the excuse that this was God's way of answering his prayers; of making his family whole; of making them, the Francises, a complete family . . . a perfect family.

"I waited through six girls, and God finally gave me a son. My crowning glory" Tan said to himself, as he smiled triumphantly.

He smiled at his reasoning, but more so at what he deemed a keen ability to make reason out of that which nobody else could find justifiable.

Tan watched as his wife fawned and coo'ed over the gurgling child. It was that instant that reminded him of why he had chosen Angeline as a wife. His mind raced back to the late fifties and what drove him to the Milledge homestead in the first place.

Tan recalled that word had long been out about the Milledge family, and especially the Milledge girls. With no daddy there to protect their female interest it was common knowledge that that was the house the local men frequented. On leave from an overseas tour, Tan Francis noticed one of the Milledge girls at the Sugar Shack, a local juke joint far enough back in the swampy woods of the Carolina low country that it was out of reach of both law and morality. Tan remembered, even now, how he had longed for a woman as pretty as Josephine Milledge. She was the trophy he wanted to take home to show that he had achieved something in life---a strikingly beautiful almost mulatto who would, no doubt, make him strikingly beautiful children; children whose faces would not remind him so much of his own; children whose hair would cause people to 'ooh and aah'. But like Tan, there was a slew of men waiting in line just to get the chance to touch Josephine Milledge. By the time Tan mustered the courage to call on Josephine he realized that he was too late. Ben Tracey had beat him to the punch.

At the Millege household, though, he met Josephine's oldest sister---a warm and nurturing mother figure. As he approached his mid twenties, Tan thought of an adage he had heard his grandmother preach time and again: 'Don't place your hat so high you can't reach it' he had remembered her saying. While Tan couldn't be certain that he fully understood what his grandmother was saying when he was a child, upon meeting Angeline Milledge the saying earned clarity in his mind. As he compared Josephine and her eldest sister, the adage's meaning became crystal clear to Tan. One of these women, he accepted in December of 1959, was simply too far out of his reach for him to set his sights on; the other, however, was not only attainable, but was far more practical. It was then that he thought that in pursuing someone as pretty as Josephine Milledge, maybe he had, indeed, placed his hat out of his own reach.

Reason informed Tan that it was time. . . past time, for his generation, to think in more practical terms. He came to terms with the notion that it was time he give serious consideration to the kind of woman who would make a good reliable wife and one who would mother all the children he wanted. Angeline Milledge was the obvious choice, and so he courted her, and by the time she was nineteen years old and he was twenty-five, they were well on their way to having the house full of children he had longed for.

Unlike her sisters, Angeline was steady and predictable. More than anything, she was grateful. Tan knew he was doing his wife a favor in plucking her from a place of destitution and shame. He knew that his marriage to her was what brought her up to the standard of being a lady. Not only that, Tan was absolutely assured that it was his U. S. Army uniform that legitimized both he and his young bride, but that it was also his uniform that served the purpose of granting his wife the unspoken status of being a military wife.

Daniel Tanner Francis knew also that being a wife, and a military wife, to boot, placed Angeline head and shoulders above every other living soul in her family. In return for such a place of prominence he was fully assured of his wife's obedience and loyalty . . . no matter what!

It was precisely the predictability of his home and the unquestioning allegiance of his wife that afforded Tan the freedom and courage to revisit failed conquests.

Tan noticed that although his sister in law had married well, Josephine Milledge Tracey couldn't seem to remove herself from a life of cunning and infidelity. Josephine's shenanigans in the absence of her husband were flagrantly shameful and served as a source of embarrassment for Angeline, Jessie, and for the Tracey family.

As he looked at the child that was unquestionably his own, Tan remembered that he felt pangs of guilt as he returned home some nights. He had been happy on those evenings when he crawled into bed and found his wife already asleep. He felt badly that he couldn't seem to help himself. He was always angry at himself afterward, yet while he was there, he would remember feeling like he was on top of the world---he felt happy; he felt young; he felt vibrant, and yet he knew he could never own her like he owned her sister. He wanted to own her; he wanted her to need him like Angeline needed him; he wanted her to be beholden to him like Angeline was beholden to him; he wanted to conquer her. . . but he never could.

Tan was brought back to the present by the sound of the baby's soft plash. To his wife's utter surprise he reached for the child. "Oh gracious! Is there a storm com'in or someth'in?" Angeline asked sarcastically.

"Oh, hush up woman, and gimme' that child" Tan ordered. Tan noticed the look on his wife's face. It suggested something out of the ordinary, but Tan knew, without a doubt, that there would never be a discussion about his out of character behaviors, so he didn't worry. Although the discussion was never had and would never be had Tan knew his wife knew.

"This is a boy, Angeline. It's my job to make him a man from day one. Them girls are yours to worry about; you let me worry about our son" Tan offered.

Tan looked into his son's almost hazel eyes and the boy looked up at him with a knowing gaze in his eyes. He searched for likenesses of the child with his mother and, disappointedly, he could barely find any. Those few that he found---his eye color; that arch of his thick eyebrows; the head full of silky hair---he relished with his whole heart

Tan smiled at the child and to himself. He fed the baby and burped him across his left shoulder as he had seen Angeline do for the last thirteen years with their daughters. Daniel looked up at his daddy, and Tan gave the four-month old child his charge: "Son, you're the one. You're next in line and, well . . . I hope you can do better than your daddy and your granddaddy put together. I'm 'a teach you son. I'm 'a make sure you a better man than either of us. You the one that's gon' bring grace to the Francis name. You gon' *be* somebody!"

Chapter 5

Daniel Tanner Francis, II was born on August 8th 1971, rounding out the seventh of his parents' seven children--- the last child; a seventh child; the only boy; a special child; their golden child; a couple's last chance to continue the legacy of the Francis name for generations to come. All these things marked this child as one for and to which great things would happen. The Francis family clustered in close to this seventh child with protective hearts, protective arms, protective ears---- protecting him from the very family that had decided his fate while he was still in the womb. While both Tan and Angeline were painfully aware of the Milledge family's inability to honor familial boundaries, they had hoped the family's management of Daniel would not become troublesome. Unfortunately, however, they had minor experiences early on that would inform them of the lengths they would have to go to secure Angeline's sisters' respect for them as Daniel's parents. These scrapes also served as a reminder of Angeline's concerns about her sisters' ability or inability to honor their oath of secrecy regarding Daniel's real mother.   Angeline's only hope was that she knew the family would never do or say anything that would, in any way, implicate Josephine. Angeline drew at least minimal comfort in the knowledge that, even as much as some of them resented her, they all wanted for Josephine's safety. This, she had come to depend on, would be what would prevent her sisters from revealing Daniel's maternity to him.

Still, when Angeline came in from work one evening to find her home inundated with an unsavory element, she was not happy.

"Hey auntie, how you do'in?"

Before she could respond to Jevonica and Shaniqua's greeting, Angeline was taken aback by the four liter-sized bottles of Coke, the fifth of Bacardi Rum and the six individual serving sized bags of barbecue potato chips sitting on her white battenburg lace table cloth. Steam just about shot out of her ears when she got a whiff of the sharp and dusky scent of what she was certain was marijuana. The vapors from Jevonica's mouth, alone were enough to cause a contact high. Before Angeline could gather the words to say anything at all, her two sisters came stumbling from the back of the house, each with a can of Colt 45 Malt Liquor in one hand and a lit cigarette in the other. Their laughter indicated that they were comfortable in her home and were having a grand time. Amongst the smoke and the liquor, were miles and miles of flaxen weaved hair in either in inky indigo or brazenly blond. The women, young and not so young, also complemented their looks with long, curved fingernails laden with polished-on glittery designs. It took Angeline a few minutes to find her son among this madness. Still speechless, Angeline came to the conclusion that these people were having a party at her house, in her absence, and with her teenage son.

"Have y'all lost your mind?" she shouted before she could filter either the words themselves or the inflection with which she would utter them.

"ooohh . . . ya'll, Miss Thang done come home and she ain't too happy", Ruby sneered.

"You damn right, Ruby. I'm home and I didn't invite nary a soul in my house . . . and ya'll in here drinking and carry'in on before my child" Angeline retorted.

"Hey, sis, he our nephew, too. . ." Ruby said, with her left eyebrow arched in a threat.

Without realizing it, Angeline had grabbed the sleeve of Ruby's brand new white peasant blouse. She dragged her sister into her bedroom, while Sarah followed along. When she got the two women into her bedroom she slammed the door as the two teenage girls attempted to also enter the room. Angeline grabbed the door knob with her arm serving as a barrier to block her nieces' entrance into the bedroom.

"This conversation is for adults" Angeline declared to her nieces.

"They grown . . ." both Sarah and Ruby protested in unison. Before they could gain any ground in their argument Angeline had locked the two younger women out and was well into lecturing her sisters with her own stubby and unmanicured nails pointed in their faces.

"What the hell is this about?" she asked.

"What you mean?" Sarah asked innocently.

"You know what I mean. I'm at work and y'all just help yourself to my house for a party? . . . and . . . y'all got the nerve to bring drugs in my house . . . what the . . .?"

"Oh, yeah, I forgot your house is so perfect, so clean . . . no drugs, nothin' like that. . . I forgot, Sarah, they don't have no liquor in they house . . . d'ese the Cleavers . . ." Ruby snickered. "Hell, we just came over to see our nephew. You don't let him come near none a' us, so we decide to come and see him ourself . . . make sure he do'in all right, you know. . ." Sarah offered.

"Yeah, he still a member 'a this family, you know. You act like we gon' eat him or somethin'. . . that boy is family . . . he b'long to all a' us" Ruby added in support of her sister.

Angeline realized what they were doing and she was not going to allow herself to be manipulated by these two women. She loved her sisters, but she was all too familiar with their games. She had determined fourteen years ago that she was not going to give them that kind of power over her.

"Get out! Now! Both a' ya'll! Get the hell out a' my house now!"

"Oh, you think you all dat?" Ruby asked, then added with a snicker, " . . . she don't even know da' half".

Before Ruby finished her slur, Angeline was standing at the kitchen door with her left hand on the knob. Her right hand made a sweeping motion through the open door to signal the uninvited guest that they should exit . . . immediately!

Angeline's sisters and her two nieces complied, however not without their share of mumbling and grumbling.

After their departure, Angeline went to Daniel's bedroom where he lay stretched face down across his bed. She wasn't sure what, but she was certain he was under the influence of something . . . some substance that a fourteen year old had no business consuming. She shook her head, but headed back to the dining room. After cleaning the table of her family's debris and washing her table cloth, she opened the dining room and kitchen windows, and sprinkled cinnamon into a pot of boiling water to offset the stench of weed, liquor, and cigarette smoke. Before Angeline could get settled enough to figure out what to do about her son who had been drinking even before this event, her phone rang.

"I figured they would call you" she said.

"Yep, they did. Are you okay?" Jessie asked.

"I'm fine now . . . once I put them out'a my house . . ."

Before Angeline could think of anything else to say, her brother started his routine apology for his other sisters' behaviors.

"Listen, Jessie, these are grown people. These are women . . . with their own lives, and their own homes. You need to stop making excuses for them. You need to stop apologizing for them when they do stupid things. . ."

"I know, sis, but they're family; we're all family; remember we're all each other had. Mama said we have to always stick together and . . ."

Before her brother got too far in what Angeline and Tan had jokingly come to call his 'love thy neighbor' spiel, Angeline cut him off at the pass.

". . . listen, Jessie, those heifers came in my house and brought liquor and drugs. I don't know what all they gave my child, but right now he's in that room knocked out like a skid row bum. I don't know what all he got in his system . . ."

". . . you're right, Angeline . . . they're wrong for doing that . . . for bringing drugs in your house . . . but you know them . . . you know how they go, and you know they love that boy; all of us love that boy. You know they wouldn't do nothin' to hurt him".

Before she realized it, Angelina found that her voice had risen a couple of octaves above what was normal for her, and certainly a couple of octaves above how she would ever speak to Jessie.

"Well tell me one thing, Jessie, how you gon' feel if Sarah and Ruby come in yo house and give yo children drugs? Huh? Answer that, Jessie!"

After more than seventeen seconds of dense silence, Jessie Milledge bid his eldest sister a good evening and offered to check on her in a few days.

By the time she hung up the phone Angeline was shaking. She wasn't sure if it was anger, nerves, fear, fatigue, or what. She feared what was going on with Daniel. She knew this wasn't his first exposure to alcohol. He had come home far too many times reeking of liquor. She had seen his little twelve year old body stumble and wobble around the house after his daddy complained about missing bottles of liquor. She and Tan had come to grips with the reality that Daniel might be drinking so they gave away all the liquor they had accumulated over the years. Were she to be completely honest with herself, Angeline would have to admit, too, that there was a good probability that her son was dabbling in drugs as well. She didn't know what kind of drugs, but she wasn't blind. She saw the kinds of friends he hung out with, and she saw that glazed over look that seemed to have become a defining feature of Daniel Francis. Although he had not gotten into any legal trouble, she feared that it was only a matter of time.

Angeline feared what her sisters may have told Daniel, or worse, what they may have told their own children, and what of it would get back to Daniel. She shook her head as her mind replayed the images of her two nieces, Jevonica and Shaniqua. "Hussies" she said out loud. "Just two hussies. . . Lord, how they mama mess up those two kids . . . don't want noth'in in life . . . just give'm a weave and some false eyelashes and they happy . . ." she was shaking her head when she heard the back screen door slam.

"You in here talk'in to yourself again, woman?" Tan asked.

Angeline smiled and grunted to herself. "Yeah, I guess so".

"I tell ya', you gett'in old, girlie . . . gon' have to put you in one a' dem old folks home" Tan joked.

While his parents were amidst a much-needed laugh, Daniel appeared in the kitchen. Sheet creases marked his face and his eyes were still blood shot from whatever he had used earlier. He appeared dazed, but lucid, as if he had been stunned into a wakeful state for which he was not completely ready. His parents noticed his appearance and shot one another a concerned look. Daniel caught his parents' eye conversation and knew they were talking silently about him. He quietly took a giant bag of chips from the cabinet and headed, in his usual non-threatening manner, back to his bedroom.

"Tan, we gotta' do someth'in" Angeline ordered sternly but in something just above a whisper.

"Yeah. . ." he sighed ruefully, ". . . I'll go down to the school tomorrow and talk to them folks . . . see if they got a ROTC program they can put him in".

Chapter 6

"No son, we're not going to the funeral" Tan declared without either apology or explanation.

"I don't understand! That's mama's sister . . . your sister-in-law; that's my aunt. She's family . . . close family. Why wouldn't you go to your own sister-in-law's funeral . . . that's just strange" Daniel argued.

"You can call it whatever you want son, but this family is not going to the funeral and that's that".

Daniel had never known his father to have been so heavy-handed about an issue. If anything, his parents had always been rather liberal in their parenting. He was pretty sure, in fact, that he had far more freedoms than most of his peers, and by far more than his six sisters. And, even though he suspected that Tan and Angeline knew he was drinking, they still allowed him to go about his own business.

". . . and here they are now . . . now that I'm close to being grown . . . and they want to tell me what I will and will not do?!" he thought defiantly.

"Can I talk to mama?" Daniel asked.

In the quiet that ensued between Daniel Francis, Sr. and his teenage son, the latter mulled over in his mind what seemed absurd. It just didn't make sense to him. And although he had never openly defied his parents . . . not ever, he was finding it difficult to go along with this edict that he not attend his own aunt's funeral. As a matter of fact, Daniel wasn't even sure how his parents got the impression that he was even asking permission to attend. He was merely letting them know that he was going to his Aunt Josephine's funeral. He wasn't even sure why he was going, he thought. All he knew is that he felt compelled to go, and since he had spoken with Jevonica, he had planned to ride along with her. That way, he decided, he would get to pay his last respects to a family member and wouldn't have to be stuck in the back seat of a car listening to his parents' woe-is-me stories of adulthood responsibilities.

While waiting for his mother to come to the phone, Daniel pondered what he found to be some strange family responses around Aunt Josephine's death. He made a mental note that he had even gone so far as to call his favorite of his six sisters when he'd heard about their aunt's untimely death, and that Jessie had given him more family history in half hour than he'd known in seventeen years.

"Yeah, that is too bad about Aunt Josephine, June" Jessica had apologized. She then went on to explain they hadn't seen much of Aunt Josephine in the last fifteen or so years. She declared that she, herself, must have been a pre-schooler when she had last seen their mother's sister that everybody described as strikingly beautiful. Now that she was away at college, she didn't feel the level of connection to make the round trip home for the funeral. Even Jessica expressed her surprise, though, that their parents hadn't called either she or her twin sister, Jackie about the death.

"I know", Daniel declared.   "I live in the house here and I heard about Aunt Josephine's death from Jevonica".

"Oh, Lord, June! Does mama know you're hanging out over at Aunt Ruby's?" Jessica asked, switching the subject.

"Not exactly" Daniel answered without further explanation.

"Well little brother, just be careful with them . . . they always got some kind'a foolishness going on, and truth be told, baby brother, that bunch over there is trouble with a capital 'T'. We may not want to admit that because they're family, but let's face it, they just don't want noth'in" Jessica warned.

"C'mon Jess, they mean well" Daniel whined.

"Mean well?! You see anybody over there about to go to work? Any of 'em over there want anything in life except a beer on Friday night and some weave in their hair?"

"Okay Jess, don't go there.   They're still family".

"June I get that. I get that they're family, but just because they're family does that mean you got to follow them down that path?" Jessica challenged.

". . . and what path is that?" Daniel retorted, becoming irritated with his sister's condescending tone.

"The one that leads to nowhere, Daniel!"

Jessica was feeling frustrated with Daniel, and at the same time, fearful about her brother's choice of associates. She didn't want to sound like her mother, though, so she exhaled slowly and made a conscious effort to control her voice tone.

"Just be careful over there, and. . . well. . . you know Mama don't exactly see eye-to-eye with some of Aunt Sarah and Aunt Ruby's ways".

"Oh, I know that's the truth, alright!" Daniel laughed.

Daniel and his sister's conversation about the ins and outs between their mother and their aunts served as a good diversion. It allowed both of them to reflect on some family issues that even they, as children thought to be frivolous and laughable. In this line of conversation Daniel realized how much he had missed Jessica. While all his sisters catered to his every whim and treated him special, it was Jessica who treated him like a peer. With Jessica he was just 'June', which had been shortened from Junior, to Junie, then to June. He and Jessica fought like cat and dog growing up, but he knew she would always have his back. He knew he could count on her to give him the pot by the handle; she would fight for him as well as fight with him. She was probably the only one of his immediate family members who accorded him the respect of being responsible for his actions, and as weird as it sounded, even as a teenager, he appreciated her brand of honesty. He appreciated that she was not always covering for him or taking him out of the decision making loop for his own life. Daniel recognized that his parents and his other sisters were being protective, but he resented their thinking that he always needed protecting. He liked that Jessica didn't protect him.

As he and Jessica chatted, they both came to the realization that Daniel had never met his mother's youngest sister. Although baffled by this fact, Jessica surmised that although she vaguely remembered seeing her when she was very young, she was assured that she had seen Aunt Josephine at least once. In fact she was sure of it because she had an image in her mind of what she looked like. She could recall seeing the woman to whom she had assigned the color 'beige' once she learned that word. She remembered the long thick almost blond hair that framed her face and cascaded past her shoulders. Jessie remembered the striking difference between Aunt Josephine's peach colored skin and her almost black and naturally arched eyebrows. She remembered the narrow face with the full pink lips. Yes, she was sure she had seen the exquisitely beautiful woman and that what she saw, even as a young child, was awe inspiring and memorable. Jessie guessed, further, that by the time Daniel came along, Aunt Josephine and her husband, Uncle Ben must have been reassigned to an army post some ways from Bristol Creek.

All the way up at Boston College, Daniel could somehow feel Jessica's confusion; he could imagine her shrugged shoulders; he could just about see her contort her face at this tidbit of fact. In that moment both Daniel and Jessica thought it strange, given the Milleges' close knit structure, that in fifteen years there had never been an opportunity for one of Angeline's children to have met one of Angeline's sisters. They both found it intriguing that these two paths had never found a reason to cross. Daniel added to the intrigue when he declared that he had never heard his parents speak of Aunt Josephine, but rather that all he'd ever heard of her came from Aunt Sarah or Aunt Ruby or their daughters.

"According to Jevonica and them, Aunt Josephine don't even have a family; she's just out there all by herself. Man that's got to be pretty bad" Daniel offered by way of seeking out confirmation of what he'd heard from sources he wasn't altogether sure he could trust.

"She had a husband, but I think they got a divorce a long time back. She had a son, too, but I believe he died a few years back . . . suicide, if I remember . . ." Jessica trailed off.

"Damn, Jess. You mean somebody in our immediate family committed suicide? How come I never heard of any of this stuff?" Daniel asked.

". . . mmmmhhh, June, you were pretty young when all this stuff happened. In fact I think Benjy . . . that's the son . . . couldn't have been no more than 13 or 14 when he hung himself. That wasn't that long ago . . . maybe about four or so years back . . . maybe five, I can't be sure" Jessie admitted. She sighed loudly, then continued.

". . . It was a pretty sad situation. Anyway, everything fell apart after that. Aunt Josephine's husband had already left her . . ."

Jessica sighed another deep sigh then proceeded to tell her brother what she knew of their recently deceased aunt.

"I'm not sure of all the details, but I believe she just never recovered from the divorce, then, the suicide. She's been in some kind of nursing facility for the last few years I believe . . ."

"What?!" No! Jess, I am *not* believing that! No way, one of Mama's sisters would've ever lived or died in a nursing home. I don't buy that one at all. Hell, mama is only fifty, so Aunt Josephine had to be on the sunny side of forty. This ain't mak'in a bit a' sense, sis".

"I could have some of the facts mixed up, June, but that's the big picture" Jessica concluded.

Because his aunts spoke of her often, but only superficially, Daniel had assumed the lack of conversation about Josephine in the Francis household was due to the age differences between his mother and the next to the youngest of her siblings. Daniel was aware that a six -year difference between siblings could be significant in determining family roles, family

position, and deference. The age spread between he and some
of his own sisters made it difficult for them to connect as
siblings.   His older sisters, Angela, Nina, and Erica, for
example seemed off-limits to him as siblings.   They were right
around seven to ten years older than him and he could barely
even remember living in the same household with them. Even
to this day, he couldn't consider his relationship with them
reminiscent of sibling relationships.   So, that, he reasoned,
could very well be why there had been so little contact between
his mother and her youngest sister.

It was precisely because he had never met his Aunt Josephine,
though, and had never heard his parents speak of her in any
significant way, that his curiosity was even more piqued.
Now, however, he was more than concerned with what he
considered an edict from his father.

"Daddy, is Mama there? Let me talk to Mama" Daniel asked,
then demanded. He realized that he had become annoyed that
his father had ignored his initial request to speak with her.

"She gon' tell you the same thing, son" Tan said flatly.

"Can I talk to mama, please" Daniel pleaded.

Without a single word, Tan simply handed his wife the phone.

"Hey honey. How are you doing?" Angeline asked in a tone
too chipper to be authentic.

"Mama, what's up with daddy?   Is he getting senile or
somethin'?"

"What do you mean, sweetie?" Angeline asked, feigning
ignorance.

As Angeline danced around the issue of Josephine's funeral
with her son, Tan gave his wife a piercing stare. The unspoken
message was clearly that he expected her unyielding support
now, as always. Angeline's nod assured her husband that her

support, whether she agreed with his orders or not, was a given. She had never allowed their children to divide them, and she wouldn't start now. In this instance, however, Angeline agreed with Tan only about one hundred percent. She feared what might get said or overheard at Josephine's funeral. After all, her sister was gone now.

". . . no need for this family to protect a person that couldn't be hurt, right?" she reasoned.

Angeline had nothing to fall back on should her family renege on their oath of silence that was now moot as far as they were concerned. Angeline recalled that in taking Josephine's ill-gotten son, she was aimed at saving her sister's life, if not the integrity of her sister's marriage. As the years progressed, her goal became more about saving her son. She did not want him to see himself as the product of an illicit affair. . . as a bastard sprung from Tan and Josephine unbridled lust and selfish disregard for their marriage vows. She wanted Daniel to always be assured of who he was: the only son of Tan and Angeline Francis; a child wanted and loved; a child who held no accountability for the acts of two wanton adults. Angeline never wanted her youngest child and only son to doubt or question his identity or his worth.

In keeping Daniel out of harm's way, which in this case would be her very own family, Angeline doubted that her sisters could or would see her perspective. They tended to see Daniel as 'the family's child'; they believed Daniel belonged to all the Milledges, and now that Josephine had passed away, she suspected they would cleave even more desperately to all they had left of their youngest sister.

Also, both Ruby and Sarah were in poor health. Angeline couldn't be sure what either of them might have told their children, and she had no doubt that her sisters' children felt no duty to protect her or her children.

"Son, I don't understand why you would want to attend the funeral of some woman you don't even know . . . you've never even seen her; never spoken to her" Angeline reasoned with her son.

"Ma, she's not just 'some woman' . . . she's my aunt! . . . she's your sister, for God sake?" Daniel fairly shouted.

"Watch your mouth, Daniel. I don't care how old you get, I'm still the mama and you still the child . . . got it?"

"Yes, ma'am. I don't mean any disrespect. I'm just surprised to hear you sound so callous . . . about your own sister . . . your baby sister, at that . . . this is just taking me by surprise, that's all. I mean, if anybody, you're a family person . . . its all about family for you . . . I'm just surprised to hear you talk like this, that's all" Daniel conceded.

"Son, I love my sister. I love all my sisters . . . even the one's I prefer not to be around . . ."

Before his mother could finish her statement Daniel shot a question.

". . . did you prefer not to be around Aunt Josephine . . . you know . . . like Aunt Sarah and Aunt Ruby?"

"No. no. Its not like that at all. Josephine had her own life . . . with her husband and their son, you know. Her husband was in the military like your daddy, but she only had one child, so they usually lived wherever Ben . . . that's her husband's name. . . they lived wherever Ben was assigned. So, she was gone a lot" Angeline offered in the way of an explanation.

"So, did y'all not keep in touch over the years? . . . you know, write letters? . . . send Christmas and birthday cards? . . . stuff like that? . . . maybe call every once in a while?" Daniel asked.

"Boy, don't be so nosey, hear!" Angeline reprimanded jokingly, but she never answered her son's questions.

Daniel listened to his mother's lame display of emotions along with her lame story of why it shouldn't matter that she wasn't attending her own sister's funeral. He noted with interest that she never once mentioned that Aunt Josephine was living in a nursing facility or that she was divorced. He found it weird that there was also no mention of a suicide or any of the things Jessie had told him earlier.

Daniel hung up the phone feeling uneasy about the conversation he'd had with his father, but especially the one he had had with his mother. He appreciated that his father had been direct with him, although he didn't like being dictated to, certainly not at this age. The conversation with his mother, however, left a bitter taste in his mouth. It was telling. He wasn't sure what the message was, but he was certain that his mother's omission of the circumstances of her sister's death, her divorce, and especially of Aunt Josephine's son's suicide was for the purpose of hiding something. For the first time in all his memory, he knew for sure that his mother was being deliberately less than honest with him. He hung up the phone and remembered a sinking feeling in his gut.

". . . damn, I've just been played!" was all he could think.

As a result of this uneasiness Daniel started paying close attention to his parents engagements with him and with their family. Because his father didn't have any family to speak of, or at least none that they had any relationship with, Daniel's only opportunities to inventory family gatherings had come from the Milledge side. For the next several years Daniel came to realize that he had missed every function that entailed a large gathering of family members---grandparents' funerals;

aunts' funerals; family reunions.   Each of these failed appointments, he recalled, was at the urging or insistence of his parents that he not attend, or need not be in attendance. Daniel replayed the mental tape of childhood and noticed the same theme: he was never present at functions that included the extended family; he was never allowed to visit his grandparents or aunts without his parents being present; he was always discouraged or forbidden from visiting cousins. Daniel noticed that his entire life had been spent under the close scrutiny of his two parents and that he had never, in his entire life, spent a night outside of their home.

Part II

---that to which we gravitate

"But there is a God in heaven
that revealeth secrets and
maketh known . . . what
shall be in the latter days"
(Dn. 2: 28)

Chapter 7

"They died just like they lived. . . together; as one . . . united in their lies and forging a path of deception . . . they didn't even look dead . . . looked like they were both sound asleep . . ."

"Well, they were sound asleep weren't they? In fact they *are* sound asleep, *aren't* they?" Dr. Matthews challenged

Daniel shot the counselor a look that would easily serve the same purpose as a high powered bolt of lightning. He slowly turned his head back to the large full wall floor-to-ceiling window that offered Dr. Reese Matthews' clients an almost touchable view of the snow-capped cascades.
"Is this what you all do? . . . have people come in here and pour out their souls to you and you cut them up like minced

meat?" he asked with every single word uttered slowly and deliberately, and saturated with anger.

"Is that what you're feeling like right now, Sgt. Francis? Are you feeling chopped up . . . like minced meat?"

Daniel inhaled slowly to try and contain the seething anger he was feeling. While there were easily enough recipients to go around, right now this therapist was poking him in all the right places; she was stoking a rage that was so intense it inspired in him an abiding fear of himself. The depth of his anger was palpable; it felt like a never ending tunnel of blackness and heat; searing heat whose source he couldn't reach to extinguish; an incendiary feeling so profound he feared he would never, in this lifetime, be able to get to its origins to extinguish it.

Daniel realized that the very breadth of his fury was consuming—he couldn't find its dimensions; he couldn't figure where it started or where it ended. He couldn't even figure who should be its reasonable target. At various times within the last few weeks he had entertained the thought of all the people at whom he could justifiably and conveniently target the molten lava that was erupting from the volcano that was his heart. Should he be angry at his parents? . . . after all, he reasoned, they had lied to him for forty-two years, then died suddenly, leaving him with the fall out of their deception; should he be angry at Patience? . . . she was the source of all the mind shattering information . . . the person who had unearthed the lies, the betrayals, the scandals . . . the very reason his world was toppled, but yet, the source of his enlightenment; should he be angry at all the members of his family who knew the truth but never told? What about the other people who played a role in his confusion---Aunt Josephine; Aunt Mary . . .?" Daniel, for the hundredth time, wondered silently as he shook his head from side to side in dismay.

"That was January. This is March . . ." he reasoned silently, then asked himself why it was that he was still feeling this degree of anger; why he was still struggling with what Patience and Aunt Mary had told him; why this information came so quickly on the heel of his parents' death . . .

Daniel sighed and conceded that there were more questions than answers, and although he had hoped to find some resolution, he was now wondering if employing the services of a counselor was a good idea after all. Already, he felt like the underdog . . . felt like he was in a no-win situation; already she was making him angry . . . angrier. . . angrier than before he came to see her.

At the moment that he stood in the therapist's office Daniel was angry at just about every person and every- thing he could think of, chief among them being himself. He was less than six months from his forty-third birthday and his life was more in shambles than he had ever known it to be. Perhaps, he considered silently, it was always in shambles and he just didn't know it. Now he knew it; now he knew for sure that his life was a train wreck. His career was in jeopardy; his identity was in question; his parenting had proven to be substandard; and he had failed over and over again as a husband.

"Is this . . ." he wondered silently, ". . . what forty-three years of living a lie . . . forty-three years of deception . . . forty three years of betrayal felt like?"

Still facing the window, but not seeing anything, Daniel completely missed every single one of the four ice chunks that blazed a path to the bottom of the hill while pummeling stately firs on their way down. Daniel was oblivious to Mother Nature's majesty as he looked at Mt. St. Helens but saw nothing. . . as he directed his speech back to his therapist, but was really talking to himself. Although his words were addressed to the counselor, even Daniel knew that he was really declaring to Daniel that he no longer knew who he was. His words were acerbic, and so was the confusion that was his identity.

"Please. Don't call me *Sgt.* Francis. In fact, ma'am, I'd appreciate it if you wouldn't call me anything at all. I don't know who the hell I am and I sure as hell don't want you or the United States Army to define me. You can call me whatever you want, but just not Francis, and just not Sergeant . . . not Sergeant anything, ma'am".

Silence pervaded the room as Daniel stood so close to the double paned wall of glass that the vapors from his breathing made a little round cloud on the glass in front of him. Whenever an existing cloud threatened to dissipate, the next breath he exhaled would make a new cloud form. He stood like that for at least eight minutes . . . with both his hands shoved deep into the front pockets of his dress green trouser. Quiet consumed Dr. Reese Matthews' pale peach colored office like a dark plague; silence haunting every crevice of the room, saturating the space with stillness so thick it hung before them like a dense black velvet curtain.

Daniel was looking at nothing in particular when words once again, found their way from his heart and to his lips. These words were in response to the therapist's question.
"Yeah. They're asleep. They're sound asleep. Both of them . . . all three of them, really . . . and . . . I . . ."

Daniel's voice trailed off as he struggled for the composure his uniform and his rank demanded of him.   He exhaled a long labored breath, swallowed hard, and silently willed the tears to not cross the lids whose reddened rims had already betrayed the depth of his emotions.

"Now it's all as clear as a bell . . . it was right there in front of my face, but I guess I was too blind . . . too blind*ed*, I should say . . . by . . . by lies? . . . by a legacy of deception? . . . or maybe . . . just maybe, Dr. Matthews, it was my own arrogance that was getting in my way of the truth. . . maybe it was my own conceit that was mocking me all along. . .?"

Daniel stopped talking for a moment before turning around to face the therapist for the first time since the start of this session. The look on his face suggested that the questions he had just asked weren't necessarily rhetorical ones.

After a few minutes of silence Reese Matthews reminded her client that they were at the end of today's session, but that she was interested in hearing his answers to the questions he had just posed.

Chapter 8

"In our last session, Daniel, you hinted at all the signs being right in front of you, but that you were blinded by . . .???"

Dr. Matthews left the ending of Daniel's sentence unfinished in hopes that her client would pick it up.

Daniel harrumphed before he craned his thick neck to the right to look out of the large window that seemed to have become a source of refuge for him. He rubbed the back side of his neck with his right hand while his left arm lay draped over his crossed legs.

"I remember her. I remember it like it was yesterday".

He smiled before he smirked then uncrossed his legs and rose from the seated position. As he strolled over to the safety of the window, he elaborated on the simple sentence.

"Private Benjamin", he smirked again.

"Private Benjamin . . . ?" Reese Matthews asked.

"That's what we nicknamed her".

After a few moments of silence Sgt. Francis proceeded with the story of how he met the woman who would introduce him to both truth and fact.

"This was in 1992. I was just twenty-one years old and fairly new to the Army, myself . . . coming up on my third year . . . but I was moving right along; had made PFC and could see E-4 coming real soon. I'd projected that I'd be Sergeant by my fifth year, and if that was the case, I knew I'd be in for the long haul".

Daniel physically shook his shoulders as if waking himself from a dream, of sorts. He walked back to the chair he originally sat in and re-took his seat and re-crossed his legs in that broadly open way that is typical of how men cross their legs. Dr. Reese observed that Daniel appeared a bit more relaxed now, even more so than he had been just two or three minutes ago. She laid down her pencil and herself relaxed.

"I see what looks like a hint of a smile on your face, Daniel".

"Yeah, you know, as I think of her, I can't help but smile. She was so . . . so . . ."

Daniel shook his head from side to side, as both his arms went up in the air as part of a shoulder shrug.

". . . so . . .?" Dr. Matthews prompted.

"She was so . . . so innocent; so green; so . . . so fresh from the farm . . . that ya' just wanted to . . . to . . . ya' know . . . ya' just wanted to . . . protect her!" he chuckled.

"Protect her . . .?" Reese prompted again.

"Yeah! Ya' just wanted to protect her" Daniel declared.

". . . *you* wanted to protect her?" Dr. Matthews asked.

"Yeah. I guess everybody wanted to protect her, but somehow, I ended up being the one that did most of the protecting, I guess. She became my own personal project . . . someone for me to mentor; someone that I could protect from the wolves, ya' know?   As young and naïve as she was she would easily have been shark bait.   And add to that she was a pretty attractive little girl".

"Little girl?" Dr. Reese asked with furrowed brows.

"Well, you know she was of legal age and all, but she was fresh . . . very young looking . . . could pass for fifteen or sixteen . . . but more important than her looks, she was just so childlike. In the wrong hands, some clown could have had a field day with her and she wouldn't have known what hit her" Daniel explained.

Dr. Reese nodded her understanding.

"Tell me about her", she requested.

"Well, her real name was . . . *is* . . . is---she's not dead.   Her name is Patience . . . Patience Bright".

Daniel shook his head from side to side and smiled again.

"She is really something.   She came in that section office green as early summer corn . . . not a hint of military bearing, even though she had just finished boot camp at one of toughest bases in the Army's training system.   She was just plain clumsy, ya' know . . . the one we would have voted 'least likely to succeed in the military'.   Even then though, there was something about her.   Something . . .? . . . something . . . I don't know . . . just something . . ." Daniel fumbled for words.

". . . the innocence. . .?" Dr. Matthews ventured.

"No. . . . Yeah! . . . Well, that, too, but there was something else, as well.   There was that 'deer-in-the-headlight' lack of confidence, but at the same time there was an eagerness to please that could easily have made her prey" Daniel explained.

"Don't get me wrong . . ." Daniel continued " . . . she was a pretty girl . . . right good looking, and all, but at the same time there was no attraction . . . none at all . . . I mean . . . there was something I liked about her . . . some kind of connection . . . I don't know . . . like a little sister . . . or something . . ."

Daniel's voice trailed off, leaving the room looming with a minute and a half of pregnant silence.

"I knew I would get reassigned before her orders were up at my unit, so I spent the next sixteen months getting to know her and boosting her confidence; you know, shoring her up to be able to take care of herself in the Army".

In that instant Daniel Francis found that he couldn't stop his mind from rewinding to twenty-one years earlier.

"Where you from Bright?" he had asked.

"Sugar Tit, sir".

"Sugar Tit?!" Daniel remembered how the section office roared with the laughter of male derision. He shook his head in dismay at her level of naivete and ordered the four soldiers who were under his charge to pipe down as he took this opportunity to put the new recruit at ease.

"Bright, I'm your acting NCOIC, but I'm not an officer, so please, skip the 'sir', okay?" he had ordered gently.

"Yes, s'.... uhm, I mean, yes, Private First Class Francis" Bright stammered.

"Relax, soldier. This is your home now. You are a part of this company and a valued member. Always remember that, okay? Now, where in the devil is Sugar Tit?"

Daniel recalled that the young private, who was probably not much younger than he was, had a southern drawl that would suggest she had just gotten off the bus from somewhere south of No-Where, Mississippi. He remembered thinking that although her BDU's were neat, her tiny body was swallowed up in the camouflage uniform; her boots were so small, they looked like something of a toy. He didn't realize they made military boots in a size three. She just looked too tiny to be considered a real soldier of any soldierly worth.   He had shaken his head in despair at the thought of the brief stature, one-hundred pound face of innocence being his buddy in a war-time situation.

"It's in South Carolina" Patience had responded.

Daniel remembered that he had raised his eyebrows at the commonality they shared, but does not ever recall sharing with the young private that they were from the same state.

"Does this place . . . uh, . . . Sugar Tit . . . have its own zip code, Bright?" Daniel had asked in that initial conversation.

"No, PFC Francis" she answered, still ramrod stiff as if she struggled to be at any position other than full attention.

"Let me give you some advice then, Bright. When asked where you're from, just give the name of the nearest city . . . say, maybe, Greenville, for example. Got it? . . . and Bright . . . lighten up; you're gonna be okay".

Daniel remembered that even as he offered his newest assignment this assurance, there was probably nothing he could muster in either his voice, his facial expression or even his posture that spoke of him genuinely believing that what he said was true. He simply didn't believe it, himself; he didn't believe for a second that Private Bright was going to be okay . . . not for a while, at least.

Dr. Matthews' light chuckle is what brought Daniel back to the present.

". . . and you should see her now, Doc" Daniel said, nodding his head slowly and with a slight smile on his face.

"Your expression changed, Daniel" Reese Matthews noted, ". . . tell me what that's about".

"Well, ma'am, I guess it just goes to show you that it's not always what we think . . . or even *who* we think. I never would have thought!" he stated with emphasis.

" . . . never would have thought . . .?" Dr. Matthews prompted questioningly.

" . . . how our lives would come full circle" Daniel offered as a completion to his previously offered partial sentence.

". . . full circle . . .?" Dr. Matthews asked, again with question marks in her eyes.

"Yeah. Full circle. . ." Daniel said lifting his right hand off the arm of the chair and drawing an imaginary circle in mid air with his index finger.

". . . full circle, ma'am! Twenty years later . . . twenty-one years to be exact, and I run into Private Benjamin again . . . except this time . . ."

Daniels' excitement is hardly contained as he scoots to the edge of the chair in the middle of his own sentence.

" . . . this time, Doc, she's on top; she's on top . . . and I'm the one struggling. Plus this time she knows me better than I know myself. This time she has to teach me who *I* am".

Chapter 9

"Have you thought any more about Patience Bright since our last session, Daniel?" Dr. Matthews asked.

"Ma'am, I don't know that I can *not* think about Patience Bright" Daniel declared.

Both of Reese Matthews' eyebrows slowly rose to an arch that clearly suggested a need for clarification.

"From early 1995 . . . until about two years ago a lot of stuff happened . . . to me and to her . . . a *lot'a* stuff . . . obviously.

Daniel looked up at Dr. Matthews as if he'd been contemplating something profound. Daniel sat with his short stubby legs crossed in its usual fashion---triangled with his right ankle resting atop the crown of his left knee. For a millisecond, even Reese Matthews gave thought to whether or not that seated position would have been at least slightly uncomfortable for her client. After all, she reasoned silently, he is approaching the half century mark and with a bit of a paunch about the middle. She noted also that Daniel was below the mean in male height. She suspected that his tenure in the Army was coming to an end and also that his less than lean body may have been a liability for his military service career.

Daniel rested his elbows on the arms of his chair and made a tent with his fingers. He then leaned forward and rested his chin in the valley between where his thumbs joined and where his index fingers touched. His two index fingers did a little dance with one another before he exhaled and started talking again.

"You know, Dr. Reese, I've got to tell you . . . this whole experience has been an exercise in humility. Although Patience and I lost touch after a few years, there was always in the back of my mind this . . . this notion, if you will . . . that . . . 'er . . . well that I . . ."

". . . sounds like you're struggling for words, Daniel . . ." Dr. Matthews observed.

"Yeah. Yeah, I suppose you're right. I am struggling for words. I don't want this to come out wrong . . ."

". . . wrong . . .?" Dr. Matthews asked.

"You know . . . I don't want to come across as being . . . you know . . . as being arrogant" Daniel confessed.

"Arrogant? . . . what if you do come across as arrogant?"

"Well, I'm not!" Daniel shot back defensively.

"I'm not arrogant at all. In fact I'm probably the most humble person you'll ever meet, ma'am".

Daniel ignored the arches that formed at the inner portions of Dr. Matthews' eyebrows.

"No, I'm not arrogant at all . . . that's why I'm struggling with how to articulate this to you".

By the time he had uttered the statement, Daniel realized he needed to correct what he was saying.

"No. No, that's not right" he said shaking his head left to right as his two index fingers tapped into one another at a frenzied pace.

"No, I'm not struggling with how to say what I'm feeling. The truth is, I'm more like struggling with how I feel; with why I feel this way . . . why I've ever felt this way".

". . . and how is that? How do you feel?" Dr. Matthews posed.

"Well . . . you know, as long as there was Patience . . . or maybe *a* Patience . . . now that I think about it, it could have been anybody. . ."

" . . . but it wasn't anybody, Daniel. It was Patience. So, let's deal with who and what it actually was . . . or is" Dr. Matthews challenged.

Daniel looked up, a bit taken aback by his counselor's abruptness.

"So, tell me how you felt, or feel . . .", Dr. Matthews continued, ". . . about your relationship with Patience".

"Phew . . .", Daniel exhaled, then said, ". . . well alright then . . . *ma'am!*"

Daniel's emphasis on the word 'ma'am' signaled to the therapist that she had touched a nerve with her client.

"We got to be real close. She eventually told me about her history; she grew up hard . . . and I do mean hard. To say that she was poor would be an understatement. No family to speak of . . . an unwanted child; grew up in foster care; all the things that were just the opposite of me. In my family I was the spoiled golden child. I knew I was loved---not just by my parents and six adoring sisters, but by my extended family, too. You know it always seemed to me that there were at least two people fighting over me---either my sisters or my mother or my father; my aunts and first cousins, even my uncle. So, there was no shortage of people fighting *over* me . . . over who would get my attention . . . or fighting *for* me . . . fighting to make sure nobody did me wrong".

Daniel shrugged his shoulders. "I was wanted; I was loved, and I knew I was loved. Patience never had that. Nobody wanted her. That, plus her being poor made me somehow believe that I was . . . maybe better than she was . . .maybe in a better class than she was. So, me taking her on as a project, so to speak, assured me of my status; assured me that even though I doubted my worth sometimes, I always knew there was always at least one person below me: that someone was Patience Bright".

When Daniel looked up Dr. Matthews noticed the pained look that had consumed his face. She noticed the knitted brows; she observed that his eyes were pleading for understanding; she heard the long and labored sigh that he released as if a steam valve was being slowly bled.

". . . and now . . .?" Dr. Matthews asked.

"And now . . . and now? I don't know, Dr. Matthews. I just don't know. So much has changed. Everything is now topsy-turvy. It's as if I woke up one morning and my whole world had been upended".

". . . upended?" Dr. Matthews inquired.

"Upended! Upside down! Backward. It's all wrong . . . like this was somebody else's life; like I went to sleep one night and woke up the next morning in somebody else's life . . . in somebody else's nightmare, really. I'm feeling like this is somebody's idea of a cruel joke . . . except it isn't funny. At least I'm not laughing. I'm not laughing at all, Doc. In fact, I'm the one crying this time around".

Chapter 10

"**W**ho woulda' thunk?!"

Daniel laughed heartily at his own utterance of what he and his sisters had long called his 'ghetto question'. Recognizing the phrase and its significance, Reese Matthews saw it as confirmation of her client's improving mood, and went along.

". . . anybody in this room?" she asked with a smiled.

Daniel shook his head left to right and answered "Nope!"

"I was her mentor and the one who literally pitied her, and here it is now . . . fast forward two decades, and the road has really taken an unexpected turn, hasn't it?"

"How so?" Dr. Matthews asked.

"I remember how me and my company laughed at her and called her Private Benjamin---the least likely person to have done well in the U. S. Army; the least likely person to have graduated boot camp, come to think of it. And now look at her; the epitome . . . the essence . . .the *very essence*, Dr.

Matthews, of military service . . . the end all-be all of the U. S Army. Private Benjamin is Sgt. Major Bright. *Sergeant Major!"* Daniel screamed the rank as he looked at his counselor with disbelieving eyes, before continuing his rant.

"Here I am struggling to hold on to my E-7 stripes, and the bumbling little mosquito wings that I once mentored is now a Sergeant Major. How ironic is that?"

"How do you feel about that?" Reese asked.

"I don't know Doc" Daniel admitted, then added, " . . . I'm proud as hell of her; not many people get there and certainly not many of us".

Reese nodded in full understanding of the racial undertone of Daniel's comment.

". . . and being a black woman . . ." Daniel continued, ". . . I know she *earned* it . . . and let me tell you, that is *not* the kind of rank you can earn on your back either; she had to be . . . excuse me, she *has* to be---present tense--- she *has* to be at the top of her game to have earned that rank. I am in awe of her. . . really in awe of her. Her whole life has been an uphill climb, and, well . . . " Daniel proclaimed, tipping his head slightly, ". . .she made it".

"So, the tides really have turned, it seems" Reese said, echoing her client's prior sentiments.

"Indeed they have, Doc; indeed they have" Daniel confirmed.

"So now what?"

"Well, ma'am, there is still a whole lot more to this story; way, way more!"

"I'm anxious to hear the rest of the story, Daniel".

"Next time, then?" Daniel asked as he rose from his seated position. He shook his therapist's hand as he walked towards the door.

Chapter 11

"So, have you had any contact with any members of your family lately?" Reese asked.

"Not since all hell broke loose" Daniel replied.

" . . . all hell broke loose . . .?" Dr. Matthews asked as her eyebrows crinkled.

"That's how I ended up here, Doc" Daniel reminded.

"oh . . . well tell me about that, Daniel".

"Where do you want me to start, ma'am?"

"How about at the beginning", the doctor offered.

"I don't know the beginning, ma'am" Daniel conceded.

"Well, how about you tell me what you want me to know . . . from wherever you want to start".

Daniel grunted laboriously as he lapped the calf of his right leg over his left knee.

"Really it was Sheila who got this whole thing started. Teenagers . . ." Daniel said as he shook his head from side to side.

He shook his right foot nervously in mid air as he started to speak after a few seconds of silence.

"Yeah, she became friends with Patience's son . . ." Before Daniel could proceed with his story, Dr. Matthews' raised eyebrows signaled him that she needed clarification on the name 'Sheila'.

"Oh, I'm sorry. Sheila is my daughter . . . by my first wife. Vickie.   They still live in Fayetteville, and Ft. Bragg is Patience's current duty station.

"Had you had any contact with Sgt. Maj. Bright since y'all were assigned to Fort Polk in the early 90's?" Reese asked.

"Well, you know after I left we kept in touch via e-mail, and the occasional Christmas card. There was that one time we crossed paths in Dallas while I was picking up my children from Arkansas to spend the summer with me at Ft. Sam. Our paths crossed at the airport in Dallas, so we met for lunch at DFW . . . mmmmh that was probably in '98 or '99 or so. I know she'd had a child but I didn't know too much more than that. That was the last time we really talked.   Over time, as is reasonably the case, we just lost touch with each other".

After clarifying some family connections, Daniel proceeded with his story of how his teenage daughter catalyzed his re-connection with Patience Bright.

"Patience hadn't long been assigned to Bragg and of course she got her son enrolled in school. Her son . . . his name is Creighton, by the way, is a year or so younger than Sheila, and they would end up going to the same high school. Sheila is a peer counselor or somehow functions in the capacity of mentoring new students through their first year at the school".

Daniel noticed that Dr. Matthews was nodding her head as if she would approve of what his daughter was doing. He used this opportunity to let the counselor know his sentiments about both the school's orientation process and also about his daughter.

" . . . good idea, right? And Sheila has the perfect personality for it. She is a good kid, Dr. Matthews. She obviously got that from my gene pool" Daniel joked.

Reese Matthews continued nodding.

". . .anyway as luck, or fate, I suspect in this case anyway . . . as fate would have it, Sheila and Creighton got paired. My daughter and Patience's son got paired. Now tell, me, Doc what are the chances . . . what are the odds that through a random pairing process of more than two hundred or so children, our two children would end up paired?" Daniel asked, before continuing.

"Well, when Vickie realized who Creighton was she called me immediately. When we were living in Louisiana, I had taken Patience to meet Vickie" . . . Daniel shrugged, then added, " . . . needless to say, those two never hit it off as friends. Vickie wasn't too fond of people with Patience's history, so . . ." he shrugged again.

As Daniel proceeded with his story, Dr. Matthews had been nodding her understanding, until Daniel's last statement. Instead of nodding the therapist furrowed her brows in confusion. Astute at responding to the counselor's non-verbal cues, Daniel stopped to explain.

"Vickie came from a long history of military men. Her parents sent her to college so she could marry well . . . you know . . . marry an officer, you know . . . that kind of stuff".

Dr. Matthews' eyes were still questioning, so her client continued explaining the strained relationship between his wife and his mentee.

"When she married me, an enlisted solider, Vickie had already married beneath what her family expected, so when I came home with what she called 'a stray', my wife was done; she wasn't having anything to do with people who had grown up like Patience Bright. Even though, I, too, was among the ranks of the enlisted personnel, Patience was not the caliber of people Mrs. Victoria Elsey Francis expected to be associated with when she married me. In fact, my lovely wife usually made it very clear to me that she was merely tolerating me" Daniel said sarcastically. "Truth be told, Vickie, as well as the Elsey family in general, expected that especially since I wasn't an officer, that I would consider going to OCS at some point, or in a perfect world that I would have worked my backside off and should have earned the rank that . . . ironically, Patience Bright has earned".

". . . got it" Dr. Matthews confirmed.

Now Daniel could finish his story of how his daughter met Creighton Bright.

". . . so, long story short, Doc, I lost touch with Private Bright, and my wife was very happy about that".

". . . and your daughter catalyzed the reunion of you and your long lost friend?" Dr. Matthews ventured.

"I suppose you could say that . . . although Sheila knew nothing of Patience Bright. She wasn't even born when Patience and I were stationed together".

Dr. Matthew nodded exaggeratedly indicating that her client's story was finally coming together.

"Right! Right! Sheila didn't know Patience Bright from a hole in the wall. She was merely an upper class mentor at her school assigned to support new incoming students. She just happened to have been assigned Creighton Bright. When her mother hosted a backyard cookout or some such madness as Vickie is prone to doing, she met Creighton and of course she interrogated him all to hell and back, I'm sure . . . 'cause that's just what Vickie does . . . and, well, you know . . . the rest is history" Daniel stated after a long exasperated sigh.

Not even realizing that he had moved his body all the way to the edge of the chair, at the end of his story, Daniel flopped back against the chair back, dropping his arms listlessly across the yellow vinyl covered arm.

"Looks like that took a lot out of you, Daniel" Dr. Matthews noted.

"Anytime I have to talk about Vickie, it zaps my energy, Doc. That woman is exhausting" Daniel declared. "Is she, really?" Dr. Matthews asked.

Daniel rolled his eyes facetiously, and tossed his head back against the top of the chair back.

"Yes, Lord, save me; only a few more months. . ."

". . . a few more months. . .?"

". . . that I have to deal with her. Sheila'll be eighteen in just a few months . . . an adult . . . and I won't have to go through that woman for anything . . .I can finally have a relationship with my daughter *sans* her controlling mother" Daniel moaned, feigning exhaustion.

". . . so, Vicky interrogated Crieghton . . . and how is that interrogation related to you being here?" Dr. Matthews asked abandoning any discussion of Daniel's strained relationship with his first ex- wife.

"Can that be a story for next time? I'm spent, Dr. Matthews"
"Sure thing, Daniel".

Chapter 12

"Were you concerned about your daughter being associated with Creighton?"

"Not at all; not for a second, Doc. I talked with Sheila, and even she couldn't understand what the problem was. Then, of course, Vickie went to the school and made a federal case out of it and, of course, Patience was notified. It was then that I learned that my ex-wife had snubbed the child of the highest ranking enlisted person on that entire base. Even then, I heard nothing from Patience, and I, of course, was way too embarrassed at Vickie's behaviors to call Patience. In hindsight, though, I believe it would have been the honorable thing to have done to at least contact Patience and say something" Daniel added as if as a second thought.

He looked into the therapist's eyes and continued.

"Plus, the fact is Doc, I was ashamed of where I *hadn't* gone in my military career compared to where she *had* gone. I would have felt pretty darn lame chatting with her and have to say that I'm barely holding on to my E-7 stripes after nearly a quarter of a century of service, while she, on the other hand had made it as high as one could go in a less time. Remember too, that of the two of us--- Patience Bright and me--- I was the one rightly positioned to have succeeded to the highest ranks. The cards were all stacked in my favor in terms of social status, military history, family support, sense of self, and even gender. She had none of these things going for her".

"So, what happened next?" Dr. Matthews inquired.

"Well, I had learned by way of Sheila, who was now re-establishing a relationship with Creighton---by the way, it was now okay for Sheila to be friends with Creighton, since Patience had some status in Vickie's eyes; she was Sgt. Major Bright --- so it was okay for Sheila to be friends with the Sgt. Major's son . . ." Daniel sighed loudly, while rubbing both his temples before finishing his thought.

" . . . yeah, anyway, Creighton told Sheila that his mother was on, or had been on, some kind of fact finding mission; that she was on a mission to find her family and that she was actually making head ways.   Creighton seemed excited about the prospect of his mother finding her people" Daniel explained.

". . . so brief me on what happened to her family, if you will. I know you said she grew up in foster care, but did she ever tell you how she got there?"

"She'd told me back in the early 90's that her parents were married and her father was in the Army, too. It seems that her parents' relationship was a tumultuous one with a good bit of domestic violence, and some extramarital affairs, too. As it turned out, after she was born the father figured out that she wasn't his biological child. The father divorced the mother, but took her, the child with him. Within a short period of time after the divorce . . . she must have been less than three years old, or so, the father died and she was turned over to one of the father's sisters. This aunt, who resented the mother, kept Patience for only a short period of time. Once the insurance check cleared, Patience was dropped off at the door steps of the local child protective services agency, and that's where she stayed until she aged out. Even back then she desperately wanted to know her people but no one would talk. As she gained the financial resources she was able to get her hands on the information she needed to help her form an identity".

"Interesting story, Daniel. I'm still not putting the pieces of this puzzle together. What am I missing?" Dr. Matthews stated, then asked.

Daniel looked up at his counselor as if she had asked him to put his head in a noose. Dr. Matthews couldn't help but notice the change in his countenance. She discerned from the look of looming fear that overtook every feature of his face that the part of this story around which he had been dancing for the last few sessions was difficult for him.

She expected that he would struggle to get to the core of what had brought him into counseling, and she had decided not to push him, but she wasn't going to give him a pass either. His growth was too important.

Chapter 13

Reese Matthews recalled having had reservations after her initial session with Daniel Francis. The forty-two year old non commissioned officer was suffering with what appeared to be a multitude of issues, some of which were deeply rooted in a troubling family history. What concerned her was the depth of this client's despair coupled with the challenges he manifested regarding the pathology in his own family system. This client, Reese, noted further, presented as less than trusting, as he was scant in his willingness to share information. The therapist recalled being most challenged by this new client's deeply rooted anger without ownership for his own responsibility for where he was, or where he wasn't in both his personal and his professional lives.

At first presentation SFC Francis was on the verge of being forced into retirement due to a lack of what the Army called a reasonable progression.   He was resistant to this option although he was willing to admit that even he believed and expected that he was way behind the goals he had set for himself.   Daniel had described the forthcoming forced retirement as a failure. This professional failure, he had noted, was yet another of his life's missteps.   He counted his two divorces and the strained relationships he had with both his ex-wives and the mother of two of his five children as just a few more bricks in that great wall of downfalls he seemed to have been constructing.

At the time Daniel entered therapy, his problems had been compounded even more profoundly by the re-appearance of an old friend in his life.   Because Patience, who in his estimation, would have been the least likely to succeed in her military life, and yet she had outpaced him in astounding ways,   her re-emergence had forced him to rethink his perceived relevance and the status he had accorded himself as a product of the middle class. All these issues proved especially corrosive to a man whose own family had accorded him special treatment all his life.   In their eyes, Daniel was nothing less than their 'golden child', as he had put it.   To make matters worse, while he was confronting these issues in rapid succession, he lost the benefit of his parents' attention to help him deal with these challenges.   Within a few months prior to starting counseling, both of Daniel's parents had perished in an automobile accident.   In fact his parents' had died in the summer, and less than seven months later he was confronted with information that even he, as he described, ". . . could never have seen coming".

Daniel Francis' first few sessions were a struggle not only for Daniel, but for Dr. Matthews, as well.   She recalled finding herself totally exhausted by the end of his sessions. His constant resistance, coupled with his strenuous efforts to constrain his emotions served the purpose of making him come across as almost contemptuous---- his responses were monosyllabic and snide; his facial expressions were sneering and disdainful. Even his body movements were rigid and mocking of the therapeutic process. All these served to demonstrate that Daniel's perception of these counseling sessions were that they were more of an inconvenience than anything that would further his growth. At the same time, though, Dr. Matthews noted that Daniel continued coming to sessions and that his commitment to attending, if nothing else, was significant enough that even this cursory behavior warranted her professional attention.

Reese Matthews committed herself to looking beyond Sgt. Francis' presentation, and embracing him as the profoundly damaged and deluded person she suspected he was.

It was well into their professional relationship that Dr. Reese, as Daniel had started referring to the counselor, started seeing the overt signs of Daniel's growth. Even the name reference served as an indicator of his increasing comfort level. She noted by the fifth or sixth session that he, for the first time, seemed relaxed enough to smile. Eventually he would allow himself to throw back his head in laughter, uncross his legs, and he even ventured at making an occasional joke. Reese was especially encouraged when her client was able to verbalize his feelings, even when they were not the kinds of feelings men tend to acknowledge. She rejoiced to herself and commended him when he felt a level of comfort that allowed him to voluntarily share with her his fears.

With this kind of growth, Dr. Matthews was reasonably taken aback by Daniel's presentation today. There was no doubt in her mind that he had been superficial in his account of his recent contact with Patience Bright. Dr. Matthews noted how he gave atomic doses of information about his old friend, but she noted also that Patience was alive and present in every single one of their sessions---from the very first session right up to today. Daniel's kind of surface skimming was not uncommon, and she fully expected that in time he would reveal more to her. She had opted to allow him to share at his own pace, however she was now pressing him to connect the dots; to help her understand why Patience Bright mattered; to put this re-surfaced woman's role in his life into some context.

Reese Matthews remembered, and took especial note of her client's expression when she had asked him to clarify the importance of a person who would, at first glance, have little, if any bearing on his current circumstances. She remembered the fading anxiety and the recently growing spark in his light brown eyes; she heard the sudden inhale of surprise, followed by the slow exhale of exasperation; she saw the upward twist of the left side of his closed lips that meant there was a question. Reese noted all of these things and realized that Patience Bright was significant to Daniel. She would even go so far as to believe that this woman was a compelling force in the life of Daniel Francis. The doctor was glad she had had the wisdom to schedule this client for a double session and to make him her last client of the day.

"You don't seem to be yourself today, Daniel. Are you feeling okay?" Reese inquired.

"I'm fine . . . I'm not sick or anything" Daniel assured. Uncharacteristically, Daniel remained standing at the door, as if he was unsure whether he should be in this office or not. His tentativeness added more worry to Dr. Matthews' already growing concerns.

"Well, have a seat . . ." Reese offered, pointing to the session area of the office.

Daniel's progression from the door to the sofa took on the appearance of a leap born of raw anxiety. Once he reached the chair he slid to the edge and rested both his elbows atop his knees and clasped his hands together as if he was preparing to pray. He exhaled a long and belabored sigh.

Dr. Matthews took the seat that Daniel usually used.

For several seconds there was no exchange of words. Therapist and client took in the moment as each eased into a comfortable breathing pace.

"The last time you asked me about Patience" Daniel began.

"I couldn't help but notice that her name has come up in every single one of our sessions . . ." Reese shrugged.

"So, I guess I need to tell you the whole story then, right?" Daniel asked, lifting his head and looking at the therapist eye to eye.

"If you want me to know. . ." Dr. Matthews clarified.

"Yeah, I need to go there. I'm not gonna feel better until I get this whole thing off my chest" Daniel declared before clearing his throat.

He resumed his earlier position with his elbows propped up on his knees. This time though, the index fingers of his two clasped hands were free from the clasp and engaged in rolling around the right and left sides of his bottom lip. This activity went on for at least a minute and a half, while Daniel's eyes appeared to be fixated on the bare top of the wood coffee table that separated the sofa from the two arm chairs a few feet away.

Before he uttered a single word, Daniel rose from his seat and headed for the window that Reese knew had become his refuge. Reese noted that this was the first session where Daniel didn't wear dress greens.   Today he wore his battle dress uniform. As he made his way to the big window, the bulky boots made clumpy noises against the hard wood floor. In this uniform Dr. Matthews could see what had become the source of strife between Daniel Francis and the United States Army. She could easily see the midriff bulge of which she was absolutely assured Uncle Sam was not fond.

Chapter 14

As if the clear pane or the view of the mountains to which it gave access was a source of strength or permission to talk, Daniel stood in that spot, fixed his eyes on the hillside, and revealed his soul to his therapist. In his revelations his voiced quaked and trembled; his inflection modulated; and his Adam's apple leapt up and down in his throat.   Although his fingers could be seen quivering in his trouser pockets, his eyes remained fixed, as if to move them would somehow diminish his courage to tell a secret that was haunting him to his core.

"She's my sister" Daniel declared in a low, but clear and definitive tone.

Dr. Matthews heard Daniel, but said nothing. She strained every muscle in her body to contain her surprise at what Daniel had revealed. In fact, she wasn't even sure she had heard him right, so she listened even more intently. Her client's announcement was so far beyond what the therapist could have imagined that Dr. Matthews found herself sifting every word he said through the sieve of her mind to be sure she had not misunderstood any of what he was saying. Throughout Daniel's monologue, his counselor remained seated as if she had been bolted to the chair. She did not utter a single word, allowing for the uninterrupted flow of her client's thoughts punctuated only by how he was feeling. Instead, the doctor's eyes remained trained on the reflection of Daniel's face in the windowpane. In Daniel's reflection, Reese could see the tension slowly drain out of his face. She saw how each line of his forehead slowly dissolved; she saw how his jaw muscles stopped clenching, and how his nostrils relaxed from a broad flare. In the sheet of glass, Dr. Matthews saw her client's face slowly dissolve from suffocating constriction to one of contemplative aura.

Given what she had come to understand about Daniel Francis, Reese Matthews understood that he would have struggled with the notion of Patience Bright being his sister, primarily because of all that would have been entailed in owning that reality. And yet, in seeing the sweeping changes in his expression through the mirror of a simple sheet of glass, she realized that it was in that very instant that Daniel had come to terms with that very fact; that regardless of how long he had carried that information around in his mind, it was only just now. . . just this very second . . .that he, at last, had allowed it into his heart. Reese saw that. She witnessed that it was in this very moment that Daniel had accepted the reality of all that he was and all that he wasn't. She saw, like she had seen only a few times in her decades of professional counseling, the absolute moment of transformation . . . the metamorphosis,   if you will,   from resistance to acceptance; from fighting to concession; from rejection to embracing. There was something almost mystical about this process, Reese, observed silently. It was as if her client had looked to those mountains and seen in them a flash of insight . . . an epiphany . . . that was suddenly life changing and life giving, all in a single instant. This, Reese Matthews thought to herself, was pivotal; this, she knew, would be the beginning of growth for her client.

"She's my sister . . ."
Daniel nodded his head slowly as his voice softened with each word. Reese noted the fading tentativeness in his tone each time he uttered the phrase.
"She is my sister . . . my real . . . my 100% sister. We have the same blood coursing through our veins. No joke. Patience and I came from the same place . . . same mama; same daddy. We're from the same place . . .Private Benjamin and I . . .".

Daniel exhaled long and slowly as if he had just unburdened a two-ton boulder off his own shoulders. The look on his face along with the calm in his voice spoke to his definitive acceptance of the words he had just uttered. The resolve in his eyes and the relaxation of every one of his facial muscles indicated that Daniel, at that very moment, had come to terms with the fact that he wasn't who he thought he was, but that he could, would, and probably had already, at least at some primal level, made peace with who he really was.

Softly, and in something just above a whisper, he spoke again.
"I got lucky and got a better life. My baby sister wasn't so lucky . . ."
And then as if struck by a lightning bolt of wisdom, he corrected his analysis of his sister's upbringing compared with his own.

". . . or, you know what, Doc, maybe I was the unlucky one . . . I had it good . . . or did I? Patience grew up with the truth; Patience always knew who she was . . . or at the very least, who she wasn't. Patience never lived a lie like I did. Maybe I was the unlucky one after all; maybe I didn't have it all that good, after all".

Still taking in the view of the mountains, Daniel got quiet, then after a few seconds, continued on a course of introspection.

"Is having misinformation and a false sense of self ever good?" Daniel asked then, suddenly, as if a thought had just, in that very instant, occurred to him, turned around to face Dr. Matthews. Although he was still standing at the window, Daniel had swung his whole body around to face Reese. He was no longer talking to Mt. St. Helens, but rather was having a conversation with his therapist.

"Doc, is there goodness in a lie? *Can* there be goodness in what isn't the truth? Can something really be good if its founded in deception and steeped in hypocrisy?" Daniel asked.

Reese remained silent but aimed her eyes directly into Daniel's. She did not answer any of his questions, however. Daniel removed his hands from his pockets and gestured as if his hand movements would facilitate the therapist understanding what he was trying to convey. All along his tone remained calm and conciliatory.

"I have to believe my parents thought they were doing me some favor; they thought they were protecting me from the likes of my mother . . . my real mother that is, but if that's what they really thought . . . if they really thought she was such a bad person . . . an unsavory element, how is it that my father wouldn't also fall into that category? . . . and if my mother was such a bad person . . . a demon, and I am of her, then wouldn't I then be, by default, a bad being too? And in this case if both my parents, and Patience's parents, too, were so perverted, then wouldn't we, the products of two perverted people, also be perverted . . . would having been the product of a man who slept with his wife's sister, and a woman who slept with her sister's husband, not make me some type of deviant? . . . wouldn't that make me corrupt by nature?"

Although Reese sat quietly, Daniel's soft sigh and his steps towards the chair informed her that her own facial expression must have revealed to her client that she was confused.

Daniel sat back on the sofa and faced the counselor squarely. This time he sat back in the chair leaving his posture fully open and vulnerable. His speech was, all at once, slow, tranquil, and pensive. There was an aura of peace about him.

"I've learned that the man who raised me; the man after whom I'm named, *is* my biological father. I've never had any reason to doubt that. The woman who I called mama, though, is really my aunt . . . my biological mother's sister".

With one arm draped across the back of the sofa, Daniel ran his left hand from front to back across his clean shaven scalp, and exhaled slowly.

"So, here's how the story goes, Dr. Matthews. My father had an affair with my mother's sister, Josephine, and I was the product of that affair. Josephine was married at the time, and her husband was on an unaccompanied tour. To keep Josephine's husband from knowing about the affair, my mother took me from Josephine at birth and she and my daddy did up all the paperwork all nice and legal and everything . . . and yes, before you even ask, my mother knew I was the product of her husband cheating . . . and yes, just about every other living soul in the family knew about this little secret. All of my mother's sisters knew about this little game, as did her brother. They all conspired to keep Josephine's husband in the dark. I imagine all the people who were or *are* in on this secret have, at some point in their lives, shared the story with their spouses and very probably with their children, too. So, by now, God only knows who all knows who I am. It seems I'm about the only one who didn't know my own secret . . . me and Patience, that is".

Daniel stopped talking for a bit and looked at his therapist as if expecting a reaction. For the first time in more than seventy minutes, Reese Matthews spoke.

". . . and what about Patience?"

Daniel released a wisp of air through his nose that was powerful enough to not only be audible, but also to cause his nostrils to flare.

"This is probably the part of the story that causes me the greatest anger and disappointment of all. I idolized my parents. They were good people, and I thought if ever there was a man that modeled true manhood it would have been my father. To know that he cheated on my mother is bothersome; to think that he had so little respect for family that he would sleep with my mother's sister is just about despicable".

Daniel paused, and again resorted to what Reese had deemed to be a position of safety---his elbows resting on his knees and his fingers now forming a tent. He rested his chin atop the tips of the longest fingers of his hands.

"I can't imagine what kind of hypocrite a person could be to sleep with his wife's sister, make a baby with her . . . then . . ."

Daniel's voice trailed off. He made a low groaning sound as he, for the second time that day, rose from the sofa and made the eight-step trek to look out into the distant crevices of a mountain whose presence had come to represent solace.

"Mama forgave him, took me as her child, and in less than a year he went back there . . . he went back and had sex with mama's sister again. He left Aunt Josephine pregnant for the second time in less than two years. Did you know she died homeless and with nothing?" Daniel asked rhetorically.

"While he still had his All American looking family to come to, Aunt Josephine lost everything. Her husband divorced her, her son . . .the only child that presumably was fathered by her husband, committed suicide, and she had lost both me and Patience. She had nothing. She died in a nursing home . . . and I wasn't even allowed to go to her funeral; none of us went . . . not Mama, not Daddy . . .I guess she wasn't worth his time anymore" he shrugged angrily.

"That's what hurts, Dr. Reese . . . that's what hurts the most . . . that he could have reeked havoc on her life and then just tossed her aside like she was nothing . . . that Mama could have known about this and stayed with her husband who could have treated her and their marriage with such utter disrespect, and also watch him destroy her own sister's life . . . and then she didn't even go to say a final goodbye to her own sister" Daniel explained in words dripping with anguish.

Through his reflection in the sheet of glass, Reese could see Daniel's Adam's apple bob up and down furiously.

"How in the hell could he have been teaching me about being a man . . . and he . . ."

When Reese heard the catch in her client's throat and saw the thin shimmering trails of tears race down his face, she walked over to the window and nudged the box of Kleenex into his left hand.

He took it.

Chapter 15

"Thank you for trusting me with your story" Dr. Matthews offered, then added, ". . . and thank you for coming back this week".

"Hey thanks for being there for me, and I'm sorry I lost it last time" Daniel apologized.

"You're apologizing because . . .?" Dr. Matthews asked with her words and with the question marks that were her eyes.

". . . well . . . you know . . ." Daniel shrugged shyly.

". . .I know I'd like to hear the rest of the story. Are you up to it?"

"You know, it wasn't that hard . . . once I started talking, I mean. Getting those first words out was like uncorking a bottle of hundred year old wine. Once the stopper was out, though, it really felt like such a relief to just get it out . . . it was healing even to hear myself say the words. It was liberating. Thank you" Daniel said.

"So, now what?" Dr. Matthews asked.

"Now? . . . now I suppose I've got to get about the business of knowing exactly who I am; I've got to get about the business of cultivating a relationship with my sister; and I've got to have a little Come-to-Jesus meeting with some people in my family. The person I'd like to have a little word of prayer with has dodged the bullet; he's the one I'm most disappointed at, but, we all know that its not nice to be mad at dead people".

"It's not?" Reese asked.

"No. You're supposed to let the dead rest in peace. Whatever they've done in their earthly lives will be taken care of when they face God in the judgment" Daniel declared with authority. Although she didn't utter a word, Dr. Matthews' raised eyebrow inquired silently about the source of Daniel's wisdom. "That's what I was always taught" Daniel declared again.

"So I take it not everybody in your family knows what you know . . ." Dr. Matthews half stated, half asked.

"I'd like to tell you that nobody knows except Patience and me and three of my aunts, but here are the facts, Dr. Matthews: Nothing is sacred among the Milledge crew. By now all of Bristol Creek probably knows. I've just got to get back there to face everybody. I'm afraid I didn't leave on the best of terms the last time".

"What you shared at our last session was a lot of information. It was a lot from the perspective of how profound, and yes, life changing it all was, but in terms of quantity, Daniel it was a ton of information . . . a lot of facts. How did you come to this information?" Dr. Matthews asked.

"Patience". Daniel answered simply.

Daniel smiled at the therapist's raised eyebrows. He was fully aware of her non-verbal cues and knew those eyebrows shooting north were her unspoken way of requesting more information.

"You're nosey, aren't you?" Daniel asked jovially.

Dr. Matthews was encouraged by Daniel's blithe mood. Her response to his playful question was equally as tongue-in-cheek.

"Kind'a . . ."

Daniel shrugged glibly and conceded to his therapist's request for clarification.

"Okay, here is how this whole thing unfolded: Not long after that fiasco with Vickie insulting Patience's son, I got an e-mail from Sgt. Major Bright. It was in my work e-mail and looked to be official. I had just come back from lunch and when I saw it I was scared to death. Although I would've never thought of Patience Bright as a person to harm a living thing, I came to terms with the fact that she wasn't just Patience Bright any more; she was now *Sergeant Major* Bright---a very powerful woman; I knew with that kind of rank she had the power to squash me like a common ant. Again, I had never had reason to believe she would be mean or hateful, but I'm not totally stupid. I understand that when you mess with somebody's child you can bring out the worse in them . . . and well, that's what Vickie had done. Vickie, in essence and said that Creighton wasn't good enough to be in the company of our daughter. That had to cut Patience deeply. Hell if someone . . . anyone . . . snubbed any of my children that way, I would not take it sitting down; I would be ready to do some serious damage to some people".

Daniel exhaled a long breath, and continued.

"Anyway I was already in this fight for my career with the Army, so that whole thing was racing through my mind, too. I was steeling myself for some kind of bombshell, so I decided I wasn't going to open the e-mail in the office. I would wait until I got home and open the message.

Even after I got home, it took a few shots of Jack Daniels before I had the courage to open the message . . . I know you think that's crazy, but listen Doc, I'd come to expect the worse . . . the absolute worst . . . I mean, I'd been walking around with this 'jinx' rain cloud over my head for the last decade or so---a faltering career; two failed marriages; another failed relationship; five children that I can barely afford to support and who I don't see but once a year; both parents coming to a tragic end at the same time; the Army pushing this forced retirement. . ."

". . .okay, I get that. Your life had come to a place that you didn't see a lot of good; you expected negative to come of any . . . and possibly *every* situation?" Dr. Matthews ventured.

"Exactly! The worst . . . I expect the worst in any given situation . . . and well, why not?"

"Any who . . ." Daniel exhaled jokingly, ". . . when I opened the message it was brief and pretty nondescript . . . something like 'please call; need to talk at your earliest convenience'. My heart was pounding out of my chest. I could see the end. The only comfort was that she provided me with her cell number. I expected then, that it wasn't a professional call. Then, my heart started going crazy all over again. I wondered if she was going to ream me a new one over that snub from Vickie. Either way, I knew I needed to call her right away. An E-7 would never keep an E-9 waiting".

". . . but you said you didn't believe it was a professional matter . . ." Dr. Matthews reminded.

"Don't matter Doc, that's just the culture of the military" Daniel clarified, then continued.

"I called her, and immediately launched into a fumbling apology for my ex wife's rude behaviors. She brushed Vickie's behaviors off as being par for the course for Vickie and quickly changed the subject. After some mindless small talk, she insisted that we meet to talk. When I tried to get a feel from her of what this might be about she was as sealed off as Fort Knox. She wouldn't leak a clue about the nature of the conversation, but assured me of two things: it was vitally important and it was urgent. She told me she was willing to travel to Washington, but preferred that we meet somewhere in South Carolina, preferably close to Charleston. I didn't think anything odd about that because I had remembered that she, herself, was from some whistle stop in the upstate. Plus, I was originally from South Carolina, myself".

Daniel looked up at his counselor as if to be sure she was still present. He realized that he had been talking a lot, but at the same time, he felt perfectly comfortable with that. The doctor seemed to be right there with him and she wasn't raising her eyebrows, so he continued.

"Now, I was really going crazy, and the down time I had on my hands wasn't helping at all. At some point I needed to go back to Bristol Creek to see about my parents' head stones and to make some decisions about what to do with their property, so, I figured now was as good a time as any. Three days later I was boarding a 747 to fly across the country. Little did I know, Dr. Matthews, that that trip would be the last one I ever took as the person I thought I was; little did I know that life as I had always known it was over . . . completely over".

Chapter 16

In the comfort, or rather, the discomfort, of his own bed that evening, Daniel couldn't help but relive the life changing meeting he'd had with Patience Bright less than six months ago. He remembered the rush of anxiety he felt in hearing the sound of Amazing Grace chiming to signify that someone was standing on the other side of his parents' front door. He recalled how his knees seemed to melt right away from his legs; how the pounding in his chest felt like his pulse would just burst right through his shirt. He remembered that his throat suddenly felt as dry and parched as the sands he had trod through in Afghanistan just four years back. Even his hands trembled at the simple task of turning the knob to let Patience in. All these bodily reactions seemed so far out of his own control and he was powerless to will them to be still.

"Why . . ." he remembered wondering then, ". . . am I nervous? This is just little Private Benjamin".

Daniel recalled how aggravated he got with himself for feeling like a teenage girl going out on her first date. He remembered physically shaking his head and jerking his shoulders before opening the door, demanding some degree of decorum from himself.

He remembered too, that when he opened the door, it felt like he had seen his mother standing there . . . a younger version of her, of course. He recalled being stunned by just how much Patience Bright looked like his own mother. He hadn't remembered ever noticing a resemblance with her and anybody he'd ever known before that morning. But, he recalled, there his old friend stood, almost the splitting image of Angeline Francis. Daniel had shrugged off the notion and chocked it up to his own state of grief and missing his mother so much.

Daniel fully expected that he would struggle in unusual ways with the death of his parents. He knew he would be challenged especially with the loss of his mother. They had been close throughout his childhood and even in adolescence. He was pretty certain, in fact, that he was closer to his mother than any of his teenage friends were to either of their parents. The only times he didn't have daily contact with his mother was during his eight-week basic training. Outside of that time they had never not spoken to one another in any 24-hour period. Even during both his marriages, and although neither Vickie nor Aisha was crazy about the idea, he had made a point of speaking to his mother every single day. Not hearing her voice...not being able to simply pick up the phone and be comforted by her soothing voice. . .had been one of his biggest challenges since her death the summer before. Daniel had reasoned then, that being at his deceased parents' house, and as anxious as he was about this meeting, making Patience Bright to look like Angeline Francis was just his grief at work.

What he knew was not grief, though, was the feeling of warmth that washed through him when he looked down at her smile and at the eyes that he had always acknowledged were just like his. He remembered feeling the same feeling of warmth and good will he had felt for her two decades ago. He wasn't sure if it was because of her diminutive stature, or those pleading eyes; or was it her petite feminine frame . . . what ever it was back in 1992, it was still there twenty-one years later--- that something that made him feel like he just wanted to protect her.

As he thought about these sentiments lying in the safety of his bed and the nearly one hundred days since that meeting, and having now a better grip on his sanity, Daniel smiled to himself.

"Yeah right. . . a Sergeant Major! And she needs *my* protection! Hah! . . . now that, you stupid fool, was just plain laughable" he said out loud in his empty apartment.

Before any words could be spoken on that warm January morning; before he could even invite her across the threshold; before he could wonder what had happened to all his nerves, Daniel found himself almost crushing Patience's tiny body into his in the kind of embrace he reserved only for those he loved with every fiber of his being. She returned the gesture and in that single expression of love and trust, two decades vanished like a thin wisp of smoke. They were back on equal footing; they were not defined by rank, but rather by love, trust, and friendship.

"Listen, I appreciate that you were willing to accommodate me at such short notice, Daniel".

"You kidding me, right? I was happy to hear from you and happier that you still wanted to even speak to me after that stunt that Vickie pulled".

"Let's not go there. We both have an idea of who Vickie is and we both know how she is. You are not responsible for her behaviors, so please don't apologize for her" Patience advised.

Daniel looked at her with nothing but love and admiration in his eyes. Although he didn't say these words out loud, the thought traipsing across his mind was pure and simple and founded in admiration.

" . . . my has she grown up; look how poised and confident she is; listen to her utter her words so definitively and unapologetically, and with such grace. The scared little girl has evolved into quite the woman . . . and quite a lady at the same time" he said silently.

" . . . and thanks for being willing to come down to the low country, and for coming to my parents' house" Daniel sighed then looked around the tiny living room that to his childhood eyes had seemed massive.

Patience simply nodded her head, and shrugged.

"Either way was okay with me. I'm glad to get to see you and I appreciate you traveling from the other coast at my beckoning".

"Not a problem. I needed to come here to get to some stuff squared away anyway. My parents. . ."

Before Daniel could finish his statement, Patience, who was sitting at the edge of the sofa with her body angled to her right, took his left hand into both of hers soothingly.

"I know . . . I heard . . . I'm so sorry". She reached her left hand up to his face and caught the single tear drop that had escaped from his right eye.

Daniel inhaled deeply in an effort to regain some composure. The sheer curtains at the window behind the sofa muted the harsh rays of the mid morning sun, but even then the salty tears and the sharp glint of the morning sun's glare caused Daniel to squint just a bit.

"Yeah, yeah. So, tell me about Creighton" Daniel offered with a forced jubilance that Patience read fairly easily.

"He's a good boy. I've been blessed . . . and he's been blessed to have lucked up on Sheila as his mentor. She's an awesome young lady. I know you're proud".

Daniel smiled. "She's my baby girl".

"So, no more children?" Patience asked.

Daniel held his right hand in the air with each of his fingers and his thumb spread apart.

"Five! . . . Really?" Patience asked with her brows furrowed, then added, " . . . Vickie?"

"No! No, God no!" Daniel corrected. "I don't know if you knew or not, but I had a child before Vickie and I were married. Blade is approaching twenty-one. Then Vickie and I married and just as we were divorcing . . .in fact we had already filed for divorce and Bam! . . . she's pregnant at the same time Aisha is pregnant. So Sheila and her brother Parker are just a few months apart. So, I've got two coming out of high school this year".

Daniel looked to the other side of the room, then corrected himself.

"Well, one coming out of high school and the other . . . well . . ." he breathed a long sigh, blowing the air out through his mouth. He saw Patience pull her closed lips in tight towards her front teeth.

"Well, you can guess . . . "he said with despair lacing his voice, as he thought about his second son. While Daniel didn't share with Patience what was going on with Parker, he couldn't help but worry about the direction his child had taken. Because he didn't want to get bogged down in his own despair, he shook off all thoughts of Parker Francis for the interim.

"I know" Patience said comfortingly, before Daniel continued enumerating his children.

". . .and then there is Sienna who is fifteen. My youngest is just starting first grade, can you believe it?" Daniel asked rhetorically, then added. ". . .soooo, there you have it, Patience. Five young'uns; two ex-wives; two baby mama's . . . and a whole lot of drama".

It was at that moment, hearing himself say those words 'five children by four different women' that brought home to roost Daniel's definition of himself as an abject failure. In that moment, and seeing how Patience had progressed in both her personal and professional lives, Daniel was reminded that this wasn't how his life was supposed to go. From where he had sprung, he thought, his life was not supposed to contain words like 'baby mama's', or 'five children by four different women' or 'ex-wives'. He wasn't supposed to have children scattered from one end of the country to the other. The script for his upbringing was supposed to have produced a show that looked more like Patience's life. He was supposed to have been the Sergeant Major with the doting trophy wife and the house in a gated subdivision. He was supposed to have been the father of the two and a half highly successful children, who would vigilantly compete for admissions to Ivy League schools.

Patience saw the disappointment in her friend's eyes and tried to comfort him with a litany of her own personal misgivings.

"At least you had the courage to try marriage. I suppose you had learned in your upbringing how to trust and share and all those things that people are reasonably supposed to do in relationships. I took the coward's way out; I hid behind my work for all it was worth. I never learned how to love another human being until I had Creighton".

"So, you never got married?" Daniel asked.

"No", Patience answered with a slow shake of her head from left to right.

"What about Creighton's father . . . are you and he . . .?"

"Creighton doesn't have a father, Daniel."

Daniel's face contorted in surprise and embarrassment. How could someone so learned, so intelligent, so professional say something so incredibly stupid, he thought. While this is what he thought, he dared not say it. On second thought, he worried that maybe his high ranking friend was being condescending to him.

" . . . is she trying to insult *my* intelligence? . . . is that the most convenient way for her to tell me to mind my own damn business?" he wondered to himself. Daniel had never been adversarial with Patience, and he had no plans to be that way with her now, so instead of saying what he was really thinking he simply challenged her in the simplest and most delicate manner he knew how.

"What do you mean he doesn't have a father? Every . . ."

Patience raised her right hand to stop her friend from going on a rant. She knew a little bit about biology so she wasn't going to listen to his egg and sperm lecture.

"I used artificial insemination" she said without so much as a flinch of her eyelids.

"You mean . . ." Daniel started, but Patience interrupted him for a second time in a matter of seconds.

"I didn't want any of the drama, Daniel. I like that I don't have to share my child with anybody".

Patience shrugged, then added, " . . . call me selfish . . . but life is simple this way. I don't knock how anybody else has done it. To each his own. There were just so many missing pieces of my own life, that . . ."

"Yeah . . ." Daniel interrupted, ". . . but don't you see that there is now a missing piece to your child's life? . . . a huge missing piece, Patience, his daddy! What are you gonna tell him when he wants to know who his daddy is, Pat?"

Daniel realized in that instant that he had easily reverted back to the old term he used in talking to her. In this conversation he was back to 1992 again.

Patience shook her head in frustration. She appreciated that Daniel had reverted to calling her Pat. Since her professional growth it was a rare occasion when anybody let down their guard in her presence. It was an even rarer occasion when someone challenged her decision or dared to debate an issue with her. That Daniel had presumed that he could call her by the pet name she had allowed only he and his wife to call her made Patience feel like they were in their old relationship again. Despite all the accolades Patience had earned throughout her career and all her achievements, she had missed being looked after. Daniel had done that twenty years ago and she had basked in knowing that someone cared about her; cared enough about her to take the reins of some of her decisions. She had loved being taken care of by Daniel Francis back then, and she found that she still loved it. So, she relished the opportunity to have had this debate with her long time friend and confidante.

"Daniel, I'll cross that bridge when I get to it; I'll deal with that when and if I have to, and truthfully, I don't think its something I can rehearse. I'll just deal with it, that's all".

"So I guess Sheila told Creighton about the accident? Daniel asked, relinquishing the topic of Creighton's paternity way easier than Patience knew he could or would.

"Hey, that's a cheap cop out, my friend. The big brother I met at Fort Polk would never have let me out of that discussion so easily. What's up? . . . and yeah, to answer your question before I forget, Creighton did mention that Sheila's grandparents had met their demise in a car wreck".

Daniel shrugged and contorted his face into a half smile.

"Yeah, I would have fought you to the last back then . . .but things are different now; things have changed. . .". Before Daniel could finish his defense, Patience pounced.

". . . what? . . . other than my rank, what's changed, Daniel? . . . or is that it? . . . Is that what this tap dancing and measuring your words is about?" Patience challenged.

"No. Hell, we're not in uniform. But this is real life, sweetie . . . and, well, whatever decisions you've made . . . they're obviously good ones. Look at my life and look at yours. Am I really in any position to criticize how you've chosen to do life?"

"Having a conversation with me is not, in and of itself, a criticism, Daniel, and yes! Yes, you *are* in a position to challenge me; you're always in a position to talk with, and/or challenge me, as I hope I am always positioned to talk to you . . . about anything . . . about anything at all. We're friends. We care about each other. I knew that twenty years ago; I knew that when you protected me not just from the predators in the Army, but from the fangs of your own wife's hateful words; I knew that when you hustled through DFW airport with three screaming children just to break bread with me. And, Daniel, I know that now . . . I know that you care about me . . . well . . . because you're here. I sent you a single e-mail and we talked less than thirty minutes after having not corresponded for . . . what? . . . about or close to a decade? . . . well, at the end of the day, you dropped what you were doing and made your way from Seattle to Charleston. You did that because I asked and you cared enough to grant me what I asked of you. Yes, you care, and I care, too, and that's what gives us the right to be completely honest with one another; that's what gives you the right to offer me your opinion and that's the reason I *expect* you to offer it".

Daniel reached over to his left and pulled Patience up from the sofa and wrapped her in a fervent bear hug for the second time in as many hours. She returned the embrace lovingly.

"C'mon . . ." Daniel prompted Patience towards the kitchen. He declared, as if she didn't already know, "You know I'm cook'in, right? Have you ever been to my house and I wasn't burn'in somethin' on the stove?" Daniel said as he pranced with glee in his feet, into the kitchen.

"Sit down . . . here" Daniel pointed toward the bar stool.

"It smells good. What is it?" Patience asked, inhaling the savory aroma of salmon baked in herbs and spices.

"It's a surprise. I bet you hadn't had this . . . well, I bet you hadn't had this particular dish *like this* since I made it for you eighteen years ago . . . right before I left Polk, hah?"

Daniel laughed a hearty and throaty laugh that accentuated the deep bass in his voice. Patience was reminded that this was Daniel Francis' own particular brand of chortle, and that when he emitted it, he was happy and excited to showcase some special culinary concoction.

"I wanted to do something special for you. We can eat right here at the counter, if that's okay with you?" Daniel half asked, half stated.

"I wasn't hungry until you opened that oven. And you're right, the aroma has me feeling a bit nostalgic . . . but sweetie, we've got to talk" Patience said with a hint of urgency underscoring her tone.

"Can't we talk and eat at the same time?" Daniel asked innocently.

Patience didn't respond verbally, but her eyes exuded concern. Daniel stood up from his stooped position in front of the opened oven door. He turned to Patience with a concerned look in his eyes.

"Pat, we can eat later; wanta' talk now and eat later?"

Although she believed the need for them to have the conversation for which he had traveled cross country was pressing, Patience doubted that they would eat after they'd talked. At the same time, though, she was reminded of the pride Daniel took in his culinary skills, and didn't want his efforts to have gone in vain. Also, Patience realized that she hadn't developed a strategy to break this news to Daniel. She wasn't sure how she was going to tell him what she had summoned him here to say. The only thing she knew with any certainty was that she was not going back to Fayetteville with this secret. So, she had less than seventy-two hours to deliver to him news that she was sure would change what he knew of her; what he knew of their relationship, but most importantly what she had to tell him would, surely, change what he knew of himself. Patience had struggled with what to do with this information for close to two years. She remembered talking extensively with Aunt Mary about this issue---when, and how to tell Daniel. She suspected that Daniel's parents were planning on telling him soon, but unfortunately they both met their maker before they could make good on that implied promise. Even then, she had been forewarned by Aunt Mary that Daniel's parents ---mostly his mother---would likely never tell him the truth. To do so, Aunt Mary had speculated, " . . . would mean they would have to wake that boy and all them children up out of their cozy sleep". Patience had come to realize that her meeting Daniel in 1992, then their children having met in 2013 were sure signs that she needed to dispense with what she knew . . . and what better way than to start the year off on a note of transparency.

"Why don't we eat first then we can talk. What does your schedule look like for the rest of the day, Daniel?"

"Nothing. Free. I set aside all day today and even tomorrow for you, babe; I'm all yours for at least the next seventy-two hours" Daniel declared.

"Okay, then . . ." Patience said, rising from the uncomfortable bar stool and heading into the kitchen.

". . . let me come around there and throw together a small salad to go with your surprise entrée".

"Sounds like old times!"

Daniel laughed and tossed Patience one of his deceased mother's old faded aprons.

Chapter 17

"Can you believe this? It's January! The dead of winter and look at this! Weeds! Nowhere else but in the low country would anybody have to weed-eat in the first month of the year" Daniel joked.

"Oh be quiet, and just keep at it. We need to do something to ward off the pounds we're gonna' pack on after that meal. Awesome! As usual, by the way" Patience complimented. Patience knelt in the delicate rye grass plucking weeds by hand from around the base of tender vegetation that were holding their own under the brisk nighttime temperatures. As she plundered around in the moist dirt, she realized that both she and Daniel were doing nothing more than biding time.

After a few minutes of small talk about nothing of any significance to a single person in the world, Daniel hit the 'off' button on the noisy tool and came and stood before Patience. She looked up into his face from her humble position, waiting for him to speak. Without provocation or words, Daniel merely burst into riotous laughter, and within seconds Patience followed suit. She tossed to the ground the few sprigs of dollar weed she was holding in her hands, and with the help of Daniel, staggered to a standing position.

"oooh, my God . . ." she groaned, then added, ". . . I'm getting too old for this".

"Okay, woman! Stop playing with me. You know as well as I do, I'm curious as hell about this mystery . . . this thing you want to talk about, so let's have this conversation" he said, making air quotations as he placed emphasis on the word 'conversation'.

"Yeah, its about time we stop dancing around the inevitable, I suppose" Patience agreed, then asked, ". . . want'a sit on the porch?"

"Sure".

They both dusted the dirt and grass off their hands and clothes and proceeded to the front porch with its gray painted concrete slab floor. Daniel sat in the glider at the eastern end of the porch. He patted the space just next to him--- a signal much like that given to a puppy--- for Patience to come sit next to him. She said nothing, but pointed towards the green vinyl lawn chair that sat in front of the huge double window midways between the glider and the front door. Patience turned the chair around to face the glider then sat down and proceeded to reach forward with her right hand and stopped the glider's back and forth movement.

"This is big Daniel", Patience said in a low, but calm voice.

As Daniel's eyes betrayed the fear swelling in his heart, Patience cleared her throat and started to speak.

"I wasn't sure how to handle this and I wasn't sure where to handle this. I only knew where I shouldn't deal with this, and that was in Seattle. I needed you to be here; near family. I needed to be here; near family".

Daniel's feeble attempt to utter words of confusion were met with Patience's wave of her right hand and a quick shake of her head from left to right.

"Don't . . ." she said, then added, ". . . it'll all make sense in a bit".

As soon as she opened her mouth to speak, an idea invaded her head that Patience later believed could only have been the work of God Himself.

"You know what, Daniel, I've got a better idea. Let's get showered and dressed; there's some place we need to go; there's somebody we've got to talk to. In fact she's waiting for us".

Before Daniel could protest, Patience had bounded from the chair and was probably rummaging through the suitcase he had dragged from her SUV just before their scrumptious meal. This was all beginning to feel really weird, but Daniel went along and reappeared on the front porch less than twenty minutes later showered, shaved, and smelling like Curve men's cologne. When he arrived on the front porch Patience was already seated there in the glider with her out-of-season Capelli straw bag draped across her left shoulder. She casually rose from her seat and led the way to the two-year old charcoal gray Infiniti Q45. By force of habit, mostly, Daniel went to the passenger side of the car where he chivalrously opened the door and held it open until Patience came around to it. Once they were both buckled in their respective seats she reminded him of the reason she had headed towards the driver's side of the car in the first place.

". . . as if you know where we're going. . .?" she asked sarcastically. He retorted with ". . . as if you know how to get to wherever we're going! So tell me, lovely lady, where *are* we going?"

"Golden Age Assisted Living. It's on Ashley. . ." she started, but was interrupted.

". . . on Ashley Parkway. I know exactly where it is. In fact I know that place very well. . . I have an aunt who lives there. She's not in the assisted living part . . . not yet. She's in the retirement village".

Daniel remembered that he had just made the left turn out of his parents' driveway onto Grayson Park Road when Patience said, "I know".

Daniel's head jerked to the right to make sure he had heard his passenger right and that's when he saw it in her eyes--- something he'd always seen, but had never seen; something familiar; something recognizable, but still not yet namable . . . a knowing, he surmised. He realized that that was also what he had heard in that simple two word utterance.

"You know what?" he asked.

"I know you have an aunt at Golden Age" she responded looking straight ahead.

"Oh, yeah? You got people there too?"

The sound that came from Patient's vocal chords was uttered through closed lips and was barely audible, but her affirmative nodding was what answered Daniel's question.

"So you found your people" Daniel both asked and exclaimed all in a single sentence. Before Patience could confirm or deny his assertion/question, Daniel went on.

"Sheila had mentioned that Creighton shared with her your fact finding pursuit. I'm so glad you found your people, Pat. Family is so important. Don't get me wrong, they can stretch the limits of your sanity sometimes, but everybody deserves to have an identity. I'm happy for you, babe. God bless you".

Daniel realized that his passenger had gone completely silent. When he peered over at her he noticed too that she seemed not to be present; that she seemed to be absorbed in a whole 'nother dimension. He assumed she must have been contemplating the visit that was before her, so they drove in silence for the next twelve or so minutes. As he made the left turn onto Golden Path, Daniel pulled the car into a public lot and put it in park. He got out of the car and walked around to the passenger door and opened it. Daniel wasn't sure what he was going to do or say when he reached Patience's side of the car, but once he opened the door, he didn't have to think about it any more---that decision was made for him. As he opened the door and squatted down Patience literally fell into his arms. She wrapped both her arms around his neck so tightly he could hardly breathe. He could feel her heart pounding furiously and felt the rapid and shallow exhalations from her nostrils on his neck.

"Are you scared?" He asked gently.

She didn't speak, but he felt her head nodding that confirmed his suspicions.

"I'm here. Don't worry, I'm here with you and I'm here for you" Daniel assured.

At that moment Patience was afraid, indeed. Terrified would have been a much more appropriate term to describe what she was feeling. She was afraid for herself, but she was more afraid for her friend . . . for her brother. Patience had doubted that she would be embraced as a part of this family, especially given the details of her paternity. She had long acknowledged to herself that Specialist Francis and then Sgt. Francis hadn't minded being her friend; hadn't minded being her big brother, as long as there existed the boundaries inherent in knowing these were titles that didn't involve them sharing a common ancestry; as long as these titles could be as easily taken back as they had been granted; as long as they could be denied at will. She doubted, though, that he would ever want to think of the two of them as having come from the same place; of having an undeniable and permanent connection. This, she knew, would negate all that Daniel Francis had deemed himself to be . . . or worse, all that he had deemed her *not* to be. Even now he had embraced her as a friend despite her growth in the face of his professional stagnation, but she doubted that he would be able to stomach the idea that they could even be related to one another ... that they could even be distant kin, for that matter.

Patience exhaled a puff of air through her nostrils and they flared in their redness. She twisted in her seat and turned so that her whole body was nestled between Daniel's crouched thighs. She looked at him and their light brown eyes met and at once four identical eyes were peering at one another.

He smiled and shook his head in amazement again at the sharp resemblance between Patience and his mother.

". . . you know, you resemble my mother . . . I saw that when you were standing at the door this morning. I can see it now. . . it's amazing".

Patience smiled and diverted her eyes towards the naked trunk of the crepe myrtle tree that was part of the opulent landscape of the senior living complex.

"Daniel, I am scared, but this is something I have to do . . . something that we have to do".

"Don't worry. I'm with you".

". . . and who's gonna be with you, Daniel?"

Daniel's face scrunched into a hundred question marks, but he remained silent.

"C'mon, get back in. We're going to visit Aunt Mary" Patience said casually.

As Daniel turned the car back onto Golden Path, he observed, ". . . that's what my aunt's name is, too".

Patience looked to her left and met Daniel's eyes dead on for the second time in a matter of minutes.

"I know".

"Now, how would you know that, Pat?" Daniel inquired.

"Because she's my aunt too" Patience said, still holding Daniel's eyes.

All at once Daniel felt the blood drain from his hands. He was suddenly cold; inside the car was suddenly cold. He was beginning to feel something eerie about Patience's two and three word utterances. Her 'I know's' were beginning to unnerve him, but he reminded himself that the path his friend was on was scary. She had said as much. So, rather than ask too many questions, he simply drove the expensive vehicle the quarter or so mile towards *his* Aunt Mary's unit.

As he neared the scenic river's edge section of Golden Age Senior Living Complex, Daniel looked at Patience with narrowed eyes and speculation that he could neither contain nor name.

"What did you just say?"

"Do you need me to tell you which unit?" Patience asked as if she hadn't heard Daniel's last question.

Daniel drove to the parking lot for the unit where his aunt lived without the benefit of Patience's guidance. He put the car in park and turned his entire upper body in the direction of the passenger seat.

"Now, . . .what was that you said?" he stammered.

"Aunt Mary. Mary Milledge. Your aunt. My aunt. Unit 6G right there" Patience said as she pointed her short, but neatly manicured index finger toward Mary Milledge's home.

Chapter 18

The sound of the door when it opened informed Daniel that what was supposed to look like wood was nothing more than a hollowed out piece of vinyl slathered with some type of cheap faux wood finish. He had not seen Aunt Mary since his parents' funeral in July, so he was excited to see her again. At the same time, though, Daniel was totally baffled by how Patience Bright would have known Aunt Mary and how it was that Patience had presumed to call her by the title 'aunt'.

To Daniel, his mother's third sister was always the one of the Milledge women that he, and everybody else in the family, held in the highest regard. Unlike her sisters, Mary Milledge had sought out an education and excelled in her career as a teacher, then later as an elementary school principal. She was always the one of the six Milledge sisters who was no-nonsense; the one with the vision of prosperity and the will to pursue it. She was the one who seemed to have always had a strong sense of values and standards. Daniel remembered that

Aunt Mary was never ashamed of her humble beginnings or of her family's notoriety in Bristol Creek, but at the same time she never let those things define her, either. Aunt Mary forged a path that commanded the respect of her family as well as of the community. At the age of 72 Mary Milledge looked well. Her hair was a mop of sparkling silver curls that dripped sparsely off the infamously round trademark Milledge head. She too, was a squat woman, but with a commanding presence. Although she waddled when she walked, her footfall was sure and direct; indicative of a person confident in the direction she was heading.

Daniel was nearly flabbergasted when, upon opening the door, Aunt Mary reached for Patience and held her in a long and affectionate embrace. The two women held each other for what seemed like an eternity, and when they released one another Daniel was floored again as, even he could not deny the incredible likeness between the two. Daniel stood in the doorway, he guessed, for more than four minutes watching the two hug, hearing the muffled sounds of their sobs, then watching each as their bodies shuddered from the emotions of this meeting. His head just kept going back and forth as he stood stunned from looking at two women who could not be anything if they weren't first order relatives. It was then that it dawned on him.

"They know each other . . . they're kin!" he screamed silently, but with his jaw sagging to the faux-wood linoleum that covered the floor of Aunt Mary's foyer. When Aunt Mary finally took him in her embrace Daniel didn't know what he had stepped into. At that point he couldn't say how, but in that instant he was certain, beyond any doubt, that somehow he and Private Benjamin shared a common blood.

"Oh my God, Oh my God!" was what he heard Aunt Mary echo as she led Patience and Daniel down a short entryway that opened to her kitchen and dining area. The large sliding glass door that covered most of the southern wall, gave the sun full reign of the room. They were also afforded access to a patio and a tranquil view of the marshes of the Ashley River. Before they took their seats at the little table, Aunt Mary took them both in a bear hug and the tears flowed again---this time from six light brown and/or hazel Milledge eyes. This time Daniel, too, was overcome with emotions. This time neither he nor Patience cared about military decorum or composure. They both simply basked in the height of the emotions that filled the room and that also filled their hearts.

"Baby, I'm so glad . . . so glad you went on with your plan" Aunt Mary nodded in Patience's direction as she blew her nose.

"Thank you ma'am for encouraging me, but at the same time, allowing me to do this at my own pace" Patience said. She then looked at Daniel and then back at Aunt Mary.

". . . ummh, I haven't told Daniel everything . . . not yet".

". . . everything . . . ?" Daniel asked incredulously. "I don't know anything! Will somebody please tell me what's going on" he both pleaded and demanded all in the same breath.

Patience and Aunt Mary looked at one another with uncertainty and apprehension in both their eyes.

"Aunt Mary, I started to talk to him today, but I thought better of it. I just didn't think I could do as good a job as you can" Patience said with an exaggerated exhale.

Aunt Mary reached over to her right and took both of Daniel's hands into hers.

"Son, I'm not sure I know where to start either, but I'm sure you know by now that you and Patience, here . . ." she nodded

towards the petite soon-to-be forty-one year old woman sitting
to her left, ". . . are family. Y'all are family, son".

Still dumbfounded by what he had seen, heard, felt, and come
to accept as real, Daniel merely nodded his head. Aunt Mary
continued.

"I don't know how God fix it for y'all's path to cross, but I am
absolutely certain that y'all were meant to meet; that God
meant for this family to be whole again. That was something
my mother always stressed with us---to stick together and stay
together".

Aunt Mary shared with her niece and nephew some family
history to which neither had been privy. Patience, no doubt,
may have heard some scraps or at least some version of Bristol
Creek's rumors about the Milledge family, Aunt Mary
considered. She suspected, additionally, that given the ill
feelings that the Tracey family felt toward Josephine, their
assessment of the entire Milledge clan was likely a blisteringly
loathsome tale of callousness, dishonesty, and promiscuity.
Aunt Mary was sure that Daniel didn't have the information
she was about to share, either. He would not have been
informed of the family history, she was certain, because
Angeline would have kept these facts from him. Beyond her
calculated failure to share her family's legacy with Daniel,
Mary Milledge was convinced that her eldest sister had very
probably, deliberately misled all of her children about their
heritage.

While Patience never once flinched at Aunt Mary's account of
the family's reputation, Daniel remembered that he sat in awe
of what he was hearing. Daniel had felt as if he and Aunt
Mary hadn't come from the same family or that they hadn't
spent at least the first eighteen years of his life living in the

same town. He listened attentively as he learned that his mother and all her sisters were born out of wedlock; he was shocked to learn of their legacy of abject poverty; he was surprised to know that his mother's family was considered to be of such questionable moral standing.

Sitting in Aunt Mary's kitchen on that January afternoon, Daniel recalled having asked his father about his parents when he was a young child. The most information Daniel had ever been able to glean from his father was that both his parents had died while he was a teenager. The most he knew about his paternal grandparents was that his grandmother's name was Patience Francis, and that she had died in 1946. Daniel had no idea that his father never knew who his own father was; not even a name. Daniel squirmed in his seat as he listened to details of his parents' existence that were far removed from what he could have ever imagined.

"Son, all we had was one another; we were the bottom feeders of Bristol Creek; the po' dunk trash of this town. As if the circumstances of our birth was a contagious disease, people shunned us; they shunned our mother. So we had to stick together; we were all each other had. Mama told us to always stick together, so keeping this family together was of utmost importance . . . whatever that was gonna take . . . and then . . ." the old lady shrugged, then added ". . . and then something went awry . . . things got out of hand . . . and well. . . here we are".

". . . so, whose daughter is Patience and. . . " Daniel turned to Patience, remembering her story of growing up in foster care, then added a second question, " . . .and how did a member of this family end up in foster care? I don't understand how something like that could have happened in this family . . . a

family so committed to . . . to . . . a family committed to family.
. .".

Daniel recalled vividly how Aunt Mary and Patience had looked back and forth between one another when he asked that question. He wasn't sure what this was about, but he suspected, at that point, that there were huge chunks of the puzzle that he hadn't yet gotten.

"Darl'in, I doubt that you remember your Aunt Josephine . . ."
Aunt Mary stated cautiously as she looked at Daniel for confirmation that the pace at which she was feeding him this information was digestible.

"Josephine was the youngest of our sisters and she was married to a fellow in the military and, unlike your daddy, he insisted that his wife travel with him as much as she could".

Daniel nodded at the familiarity of this story. It was the story Patience had told him twenty years ago and it sounded a little like what he recalled his sister and his mother telling him in 1988 when his aunt died. He raised his hand with his palm faced toward his aunt in a gesture that indicated she should stop. Daniel didn't want his friend, who he now believed was his first cousin, to have to hear a horror story that she had already lived.

"Daniel, there is a good bit more to this story than what we're telling you today, but I think we'd better leave off here. When you're ready to hear the rest. . . and you *need* to know it all, son. . . I'm always here, and Patience has all the facts, too" Aunt Mary said.

Daniel had decided that he had no need for further detail. He recognized that there was a reason God made his and Patience's paths cross in the first place, then again two decades later. It also made sense to him that he could see his mother's likeness in Patience. It all made sense, he remembered thinking, and with that, he didn't believe he either wanted or needed to hear more. Whatever those other pieces were, he decided, was of no significance to him. He had his cousin and that was enough for him. Daniel acknowledged to himself that he already cared very deeply for Patience, and certainly he respected her. His immediate plans were that he would get his sisters on the phone and have some type of celebration to welcome their dead mother's dead sister's daughter to the family.

"This is just awesome, ya' know. I never met Aunt Josephine, but I remember when she died. I wasn't sure why, but Mama and Daddy were adamant that I not go to the funeral. I was a teenager and I was kinda' shocked by their reaction. Then Jessie told me about her son . . . you know . . ."

Daniel's voice trailed off as he looked across the table toward Patience, then added " . . . sorry".

Patience looked down for a second before she returned her eyes to Daniel.

"His name was Benjamin, Jr. and I know the circumstances of his death . . . I know that he committed suicide".

"Does Uncle Jessie and Aunt Eva and Aunt Sara and them know yet? And how did y'all two come together?" Daniel asked jubilantly, pointing his fingers between the two women.

"Do Jesus, No! Son, so far nobody knows about this except for the three of us sitt'in around this table . . . and I'd appreciate it if we can keep it that way until we can get all the pieces of this puzzle on the table. Like I told you, there is more to this story and you need to have *all* the pieces before we bring the other family members in this" Aunt Mary decided. She then sought Daniel's commitment to secrecy.

"Do I have your word on that, Daniel?"

Although he wasn't entirely sure he understood why this information needed to remain under wraps, Daniel knew that he should, and would, without question, defer to the wisdom of his elder.

"Yes ma'am".

Patience then used this opportunity to share with Daniel how she came to meet her aunt.

"Creighton was right about my fact finding mission, Daniel. I was determined to find out who I was; who I am, and from whence I came. The birth certificate I had showed my name as Bright, but that wasn't my birth name or my authentic birth certificate. I was able to secure a true copy of my birth certificate once I figured out where I was born. It didn't take long for me to learn that both my parents were dead. The only name I had from which to start any research was Tracey. So that name in South Carolina led me down a few blind alleys until I ran across the daughter of Ben Tracey's sister. She was really the one who opened up some doors for me. My daddy. . . well my mother's husband's sister changed my name to that of her husband, Bright. She didn't want me to have any connection with the Tracey family. The story of my paternity was pretty sordid within the Tracey family, so they didn't much want to talk about it with me. Instead, Ben Tracey's niece was kind enough to point me in the direction of the Milledge family here in Bristol Creek. In my search I found three Milledges in Bristol Creek--- Jessie, Ruby and Mary. I didn't want to risk knocking on a man's door with these kinds of questions, for fear that it might stir up turmoil in the household . . . although if I absolutely had to, I would. Ruby Milledge was already gone by the time I was on this mission, so I turned to Mary Milledge. It didn't take long for me to realize that I was on the right path".

Aunt Mary picked up the story of their meeting from that point.

". . .I was waiting; just a waiting . . ." Aunt Mary nodded introspectively. "I didn't know all the details, but before Josephine died . . . you know she had a stroke and couldn't talk too plain . . . but she was trying to tell me something. When I contacted the Tracey family one sister told me there was a child but that the older sister had the child and out of vengeance she was never going to let that child be a Milledge. They were still angry and blaming Josephine for . . . for . . . you know . . . what happened to the boy . . . . Before Ben Tracey's oldest sister died, she confessed to the younger sister that she had given the child away to the welfare people and that's when they talked to one another about who was probably the child's father".

"So, you found out the identify of both your parents at the same time, then?" Daniel asked Patience.

Daniel couldn't help but notice the uneasiness in his friend's face as Patience nodded slowly, but with a profusion of feelings written all over her face. There was sadness in her eyes and lines of trepidation marring her forehead. While Patience's facial expression was born of her fear for what Daniel had yet to learn, Daniel believed his friend's expression was the product of her not being altogether thrilled about her paternity. In that moment he was challenged in understanding what it must have been like for Patience to have learned that she was the product of an affair; that she, by virtue of her conception, if nothing else, was, at the core of her being, less than one-hundred percent wholesome; that she was the result of someone's sin. Daniel's heart immediately went back to 1992. He immediately felt pity for his friend, and like two decades ago, he silently committed himself to helping her through this process of personal discovery and acceptance.

Sitting at Aunt Mary's kitchen table on that Wednesday, Daniel declared in his heart that he would fully embrace Patience as his cousin and make sure everyone else in his family also accord her full respect. He determined in his heart that he would not, under any circumstances, allow anyone to cast aspersions against his cousin for the circumstances of her birth. Daniel had, for the second time in his long relationship with Patience Bright, assumed a higher calling---that of Patience's protector. Daniel smiled smugly to himself, as he believed he had found yet another means by which he had trumped Private Benjamin.

"Even as a Sergeant Major. . ." he thought silently, ". . . she still needs me".

In the more than three or so hours of sitting at that table Daniel had learned more about his family than he'd known in more than four decades of living. He exhaled a long sigh of fatigue. He gauged his own exhaustion and figured that Patience's fatigue had to be far worse than his own. He assumed that this whole process had to have worn her out .

Before leaving Aunt Mary's house, led by the eldest member, the trio prayed. They prayed for peace in their own hearts and within the family; they prayed for strength; and they thanked God for the joy of discovering and bringing home what Aunt Mary had called one of their lost sheep. Aunt Mary sent her niece and nephew packing with enough food to stave off hunger for at least a week.

Chapter 19

"**W**ho would'a thunk?"

Both Daniel and Patience roared with laughter at what they had, 'in the olden days' called Daniel's ghetto reference. "Nobody in this town", Patience parroted, and they laughed even louder.

"Phew! That was deep, Pat. That was deep. How did you feel finding out all that information?"

"Glad!" Patience fairly shouted.

"It's a lot!" Daniel declared in a shout equaling Patience's.

"It is . . . but I already knew the back story. I just needed to know names and, well . . . faces" Patience said.

Daniel continued shaking his head from side to side.

"This is just . . . just . . . just, I don't know! Hell I'm speechless, and have you ever known Daniel Francis to be speechless? If there is anything I can do, it's talk . . . but this one? . . . this one just hit me like a ton of bricks" Daniel said.

He put the car in park, turned his head to the right and smiled.

"Welcome home cuzz. I have made it my personal mission to introduce you to every member of the family. I will teach you the ropes . . . and yes, there are some predators amongst us, but I'll keep you safe. In fact, since you don't have any sisters or brothers, I'd like you to be my sister; my little sister; my honorary baby sister".

In mock form, Daniel took his own made-up oath of brotherhood. He placed his right hand over his heart and raised his left hand with the palm facing Patience.

"As your big brother, I hereby pledge to hereafter and for evermore protect you, Patience Bright, from all hurt, harm and danger. Amen".

The two laughed like mischievous imps as they tumbled out of the vehicle that still had its new-car smell. Patience was glad for the cover of darkness so Daniel wouldn't see the tears that were threatening to roll over her eyelids onto her face. She was both happy and grateful that her friend was so committed to embracing her as a blood kin. At the same time, though, she knew that their ties ran so much deeper and she knew also, that he didn't have a clue of the depth of their kinship. Patience wondered how happy Daniel would be when he learned the truth.

"It's been a heavy day. We'd better unload all this food Aunt Mary gave us and get some rest".

"Go on in the house, Pat. I'll take care of this stuff" Daniel instructed, then corrected himself.

"Excuse me. Go on in the house *Cousin* Pat . . ." he laughed.

When Daniel came in the front door he found Patience standing in front of the mantel looking at pictures. She was so mesmerized she seemed not to have heard even when he accidentally slammed the door with his booted foot.

". . . just some of your family, babe. You'll get to meet all of 'em . . . even the one's that are not alive. I'm going to the cemetery tomorrow to take care of some business and to visit Mama and Daddy. I can show you where Aunt Josephine is if you want" Daniel offered.

"Thanks, Daniel I appreciate the offer, but I'm not sure I'm quite ready for that just yet . . . I think I'll need a little more time" Patience begged off, then headed for bed.

Daniel recalled in his reminiscing that even as utterly exhausted as he was that evening, there was no hint of sleep in his eyes. Try as he might, he simply couldn't get his mind to stop reeling; couldn't get the brakes in his mind to work. Late into the night he got a call from his cousin, Javonica. She had spied the cars in his parents' yard and wanted to make sure nothing was amiss. Since none of the Francis children lived in the state, it was unlikely to see a vehicle in the Francis' yard. Once she was assured that it was Daniel who was driving the rental with South Carolina tags, her next question involved who the other vehicle belonged to and who that person was in relation to her cousin.

"Yo mama body ain't hardly cold in the grave yet, and you hook'in up with some woman in her house? Boy, you know you ain't bout noth'in" Javonica accused.

Daniel cringed whenever he heard any of his family members refer to him as a boy, but he thought it best not to attempt that discussion with Javonica.

"Stop! Stop! Stop, Javonica. First of all, 'hello', and its good to hear your voice, too, cousin . . . and thanks for keeping an eye out for the place, but before you get to far ahead of yourself, let me stop you in your tracks.   It's nothin' like that" Daniel laughed," . . . but I'll tell you what, girlfriend, them eyes 'a yours sure don't miss a thing, do they?"

As he heard himself converse with Javonica in the vernacular, Daniel was amazed at how adaptable he could be in his speech. "Well, we suppose to look out fa' one another. I know ain't nobody got no business at Aunt Angeline and Uncle Tan house. You should be happy I'm keep'in my eye on the place fa' you" Javonica declared.

"I am happy, cuzz. Thank you very much" Daniel offered.

"Now what'choo do'in in Bristol Creek in da' middle a' da week?. . . dis ain't no holiday or noth'in" Javonica asked.

"Can't I come home when I get good and damn ready, woman?" Daniel asked, feigning irritation at his cousin's blatant disregard for is privacy.

"Boy dis is not yo home; yo home is some way out on the other side a' America. You don't live here no mo, so don't play dat . . ." Javonica stated, then added, " . . . now back to my original question: who is that lady in da' house wit' you? I know it's a lady 'cause I see y'all do'in the grass together and then y'all got all dress up and gone out for a long time. She must got a good job 'cause that sho is a fine ride she got".

"Dang, girl. You know how many times I went to the bathroom, too? Daniel asked facetiously.

"Don't get smart wit' me now, 'cause you know I'm older than you. You gon' tell me or you want me ta' come over they and pay y'all a little visit?" Javonica threatened.

"That won't be necessary, Javonica. Her name is Patience and she is an old army buddy of mine" Daniel confessed.

"Patience?! Wha' kin'a name is dat? She don't look white. Wha' her last name is Daniel? Javonica asked.

"Bright. Patience Bright" Daniel snapped, now becoming genuinely irritated at one of the cousins his parents had forbidden him for associating with as a teenager. As he listened to this conversation he suddenly understood his parents' trepidation and wished he had heeded their words.

"She your new girlfriend? . . . bring her over here so the family can meet her . . . see if she da' right one for you" Javonica asked then offered.

"Javonica, its been a long day, and I'm turning in now. I'm gonna' stop by and visit Aunt Sarah before I go back to Seattle in a few days. Is Aunt Eva over there, too?"

"Way else dey go'in? Javonica snapped back.

"Good. Give them both my regards and let them know I'll see them in a day or so. Good night cousin".

Daniel ended the call before Javonica could protest.

Daniel reclined back on the bed that was once his own. He looked about the room and thought how incredibly small it was. He thought how the whole house looked small. He was amazed that his parents had left his bedroom exactly as it was when he had left home nearly a quarter of a century ago. Even his adolescent posters still hung on the walls.

". . . as if they thought I was coming back. . ." he said to himself. He then added, out loud, this time,

" . . . and as if I would have come back, I would return as a teenager".

He shook his head.

He stretched out his legs and locked his two hands together and they served as the pillow between the back of his head and the wooden head board. Daniel admitted to himself that although words were coming out of his mouth into the phone in his conversation with Javonica, they were just that. His utterances to a cousin and the friend he had long outgrown, were merely words in his attempt to bide time and avoid being accused of being rude or uppity. He realized that he didn't know anything Javonica said. . . well because he simply wasn't paying attention. His entire mind was consumed with what had transpired at Aunt Mary's kitchen table. His every thought was on one thing: how it was that Patience Bright and he were family; how their paths had crossed twenty years ago and their children's paths had crossed two decades later; how absolutely incredibly small this world really was. Daniel shook his head from side to side and considered how the news he learned today had changed his world.

Daniel thought about the woman lying in the room just a few feet away from him. He wondered about the forces that brought them together twenty-two years ago and how that mighty force had brought them back together this time. He thought about the power of something mightier than himself or of Patience's rank; he thought about a force so merciful that all the pieces fell into place at precisely the right time. It was as if God knew the precise time to bring Patience into his life---- the right time for him; the right time for Patience; and even for Aunt Mary. Daniel thought that his elder aunt getting to meet her youngest sister's child before she died had to have been a wonderful blessing for Aunt Mary. He would make certain, he had decided, that Aunt Eva and Aunt Sarah and Uncle Jessie would all get to know their niece.

" . . . she's my cousin; we're family. Damn, this is the strangest thing in the world" he said to himself.

The thought of how this could have gone awry frightened him. What if they had somehow developed a romantic interest in one another, or if their children had developed a romantic interest in one another, he considered.

"This could've gone badly . . . suppose . . ."

At that point even Daniel himself had to laugh out loud at the possibilities of how things could have gone wrong. He raised himself up to a sitting position, and for the first time gave serious consideration for how little his own children knew about his family. Sheila and Sienna were the only two of his children who had had any appreciable amount of contact with his family. Even then, their contact had only been with his parents, and these visits were sporadic, at best. Whenever Sienna or Sheila visited, his parents would take them to church, where they got at least a cursory glance at some members of the Milledge family. His parents would also make sure to take his two daughters to visit Uncle Jessie and his family. His parents had never hosted any visits with either of his sons. In fact, Frisco had never seen a living soul from the Francis family. And Blade, he reminded himself, had grown up right in Bristol Creek and yet there had been no contact between his family and his eldest son. Tears stung the backs of Daniel's eyes as he considered these facts. It dawned on him that his children didn't know either his immediate or extended family. It dawned on him that his children really didn't know one another . . . and the hard cold fact was that his children hardly knew him; and he barely knew them. Daniel imagined his own children looking as pleadingly as Patience had looked; he imagined them wanting to belong; he wondered if they believed, like Patience did, that they were not worthy of their family's love.

At eight minutes before four in the morning, Daniel rolled off his childhood bed and knelt where he had knelt as a child. He offered God thanks and praises for that with which he had been blessed within the last twenty-four hours; he asked God to grant him the courage to embrace his new relationship and the wherewithal to do whatever needs to be done to bond with his own children. He did not want his children to suffer what Patience Bright had suffered. So, in this new year, he decided, he would step up his game as a father. Actively connecting with his children, he had decided, would be the mission on which he would embark on in 2014.

Chapter 20

The loud and urgent rapping at the door startled Patience out of the little snippets of sleep she had been able to steal in the early morning hours. Between her racing thoughts of all that had happened so far and the prospect of managing how to get the rest of the news to Daniel, Patience had only been able to get tiny snatches of sleep throughout the night. When she was lucid enough to understand that what she was hearing was pounding at the front door, she set about looking for Daniel. When he didn't answer her calls she thought that maybe he was fortunate enough to have been able to sleep. Rather than wake him, too, she draped herself in the thick terry cloth robe she had purchased with Hyatt Gold Pass membership points and ran to the front door.

When Patience swung open the door there before her were three women, all with some degree of features that mimicked those of Aunt Mary. When they saw her they acted like they had seen a ghost. One swooned and pretended to faint; a younger one caught the fainting person, while she, herself stood aghast; and the third one started doing something that looked like Big Bird's chicken dance, while she howled 'Oh Jesus! Oh God! Lord help me!' all the while clutching at her chest.

Patience invited the women into the house, then ran to the bedroom where she believed Daniel would have slept and knocked vigorously on the door. When he didn't answer, she came back to the kitchen looking for coffee but did not find any. In desperation, Patience called Daniel's phone. He answered sounding as chipper as a cardinal on an April morning.

"Daniel, where are you?" She demanded.

"Out getting coffee, why what's up?"

"You have company" Patience announced.

"Company? It's twenty minutes after six in the morning".

"Daniel, I, of all people, know what time it is", Patience said tersely. She continued with greater inflection on her words, but with her tone lowered by her clenched teeth.

". . .you have company, so bring enough coffee for them, too" Patience ordered, then ended the call before Daniel could say another word.

She then went back into the living room to assure the guests that Daniel would be there shortly and to excuse herself so she could dress. Before she could say anything else or leave the living room, the inquisition started, with the questions coming primarily from the youngest of the three women:

"You Daniel new girlfriend?"

"Way you from?"

"Yo face sho look familiar".

The short stocky woman who, just minutes earlier, was close to passing out, had suddenly regained her faculties. Although she and her almost twin sister had gathered some measure of composure, they continued eyeing Patience suspiciously. The obviously more brazen of the two older women boldly asked Patience if she and Daniel were ". . . getting busy". Patience wasn't so far removed from her own roots to fully understand that this daring woman, who was still a perfect stranger, was asking whether or not she and Daniel had been sexually intimate. Patience's only response to the woman's question was wordless, but it undoubtedly conveyed her shock at having been asked such a personal question. Her eyes widened in amazement, as her neck and chest turned a bright crimson. At the same moment her jaw dropped all the way to the wood floor.

As soon as he saw the vehicle in his parents' driveway Daniel was assured of who had come to call. This trio, he told himself, was not the magi; they were not wise by any definition of the word; and the only thing they came bearing was trouble.

Within the very moment that the front door swung open, Daniel's anger was clearly evident in his reddened face as well as the pulsing veins in his temples and across the sides of his head. Being mindful of his two elderly aunts, Daniel knew to tone it down; he knew that no matter how angry he was at Javonica and even at his meddlesome Aunt Sarah and her protégé, Aunt Eva, he needed to be respectful of the latter two. There was a time, he reminded himself, when Aunt Eva didn't allow herself to be dragged too far into Aunt Sarah's shenanigans. While she never stayed out of the fray altogether, Aunt Eva usually wasn't the catalyst for unrest and drama within the family. Back then, Daniel recalled, it was Aunt Sarah and Aunt Ruby, along with Aunt Ruby's daughter

Javonica, who were constantly stirring up discontent among family members. Since Javonica's mother's death a few years ago, Aunt Eva had joined forces with her niece and her older sister in keeping trouble churning in the family like a constantly growing hurricane. These three spent most of their days in the unproductive pursuit of digging up, if not creating, vicious and hurtful stories about family members, then using these as a source of entertainment for themselves. Whatever trouble they stirred up would be broadcasted in graphic and often fabricated detail to anyone who would listen. Then the trio would prompt reactions to the very stories they had made up by offering emotionally spiked commentary on them. Daniel remembered uttering a sigh of relief as Patience had told the story of looking for some of her mother's kin. He was so thankful that she had come upon Aunt Mary as opposed to any of his other aunts, especially these two.

"Thank God . . ." he remembered thinking, " . . . that Aunt Sarah, Aunt Ruby, or Aunt Eva had all carried their husbands names, making them a little difficult to track when looking for the sir name 'Milledge'".

He had shuddered to think of how things would have turned out had Patience run across Aunt Sarah, Aunt Ruby, or Aunt Eva when she was trying to connect with her mother's family.

"Good morn'in, Aunt Sarah; good morn'in Aunt Eva" Daniel said as he wrapped each in a less than genuine embrace. He eventually worked his way around to hugging Javonica, but at the same time giving her the evil eye.

"Y'all met Patience" Daniel stated, rather than asked.

The heads of all the women in the room, including Patience's, went from left to right.

"No! we just got here and she had to call you before she even tell us her name" Javonica said in an octave above what is used in regular conversation.

Daniel looked at the cousin with whom he had spent way too much time hanging out as a teenager, and he was now embarrassed. He was embarrassed by the ridiculously long blond weave that extended beyond her backside; he was embarrassed by the two-inch fingernails that shone with fake diamond and gold nuggets; he was embarrassed by the gold teeth; but most of all he was embarrassed that his cousin wasn't embarrassed by her appearance or her demeanor. He was embarrassed that she wasn't embarrassed that she had spent a lifetime of doing nothing more than making others miserable; that she was content having spent nearly half a century settling for what little the state would allot for each child she birthed. This, he thought to himself, is the element of the family he would never have wanted someone of Patience's caliber to meet.

"Child 'dis yo girlfriend?' Aunt Sarah asked in what he remembered his mother calling her 'outdoors' voice.

"Oh, no ma'am. She's . . ." Daniel started, but was interrupted loudly and abruptly.

"Oh, I know who she is . . . I know 'xactly who da' child is. I just wanna' make sho you know who she is! . . ." Aunt Sarah declared, before giving her younger sister a sidelong glance.

"Eva, you know . . ."

"Lord, God yes! Yes, I know! Do Jesus!"

Aunt Eva closed her eyes tightly and lifted her face towards the ceiling.

"Thank you Jesus! Thank you, Lord!" she shouted as she walked around the sofa a few times, clapping her hands and stomping her feet.

"Girl, when you open da' doe, you don't know wha' you did! The good Lord done ansa' my pray's . . . mmmh mmmh, mmhh!" Aunt Sarah shouted shaking her head from side to side.

Daniel stood frozen with a paper tray laden with Starbucks coffee cups, the contents of which were, by now getting cold. He wasn't entirely sure what his aunts were talking about, but he suspected it had something to do with Patience being a part of their family.

"How would they know, though?" he thought silently.

Even as he thought about what they might know, Daniel felt that any movement he made or any word he uttered would serve as confirmation, and then fuel for their fiery gossip.

Patience, too, stood stock still. Her paralysis, however, was due to the fact that she was totally and completely overwhelmed just by their guests' presence. It was not even seven in the morning, and although she was getting a picture of who these people were and how they operated in this family, she still wasn't quite comprehending what was happening around her.

"Aunt Sarah, Aunt Eva, what are ya'll talking about?" Daniel begged for answers as to what his aunts were hinting at, while at the same time trying to infuse some calm into his own voice. He realized that all of a sudden his parents' living room felt like a beehive. A place that, just the day before, was tranquil, was now a mine field that required Daniel's careful navigation. In addition to the sheer volume of their guests voice tones, there were the innuendoes, suggestions, and Aunt Eva's crying and praising. In short order Daniel realized that he and Patience were the only two not making much sound and yet the only two that, even in silence, were making any sense. This felt to Daniel, like chaos. Daniel was certain of one thing. He knew that Aunt Mary hadn't betrayed their trust, but the innuendos flying around this living room suggested that Aunt Sarah, Aunt Eva and Javonica knew something about Patience's relationship to this family. Daniel knew to tread carefully though, as Aunt Sarah's reputation as a master manipulator had been rightfully earned.

"Thank you Jesus!" Aunt Eva continued shouting as she pranced around the sofa in what appeared to be a dazed state.

"Y'all sho y'all two ain't been do'in the do?" Aunt Sarah asked pointing her fake fingernails back and forth between Patience and Daniel accusingly. She added " . . . 'cause we ain't the kin'a' people who do dat inbreed'in thing".

At this statement Daniel found his hands trembling. He had to race the five or so steps to the kitchen counter to place the paper tray before he dropped it. Daniel couldn't be sure if Patience's dropped jaw was due to the sheer crassness of Aunt Sarah's comments or because, like him, she was stunned at the implication that this trio of trouble makers knew she was a relative.

"What did you say, Aunt Sarah?" Daniel asked.

"You hear me, boy! Don'choo play wit' me!" Aunt Sarah warned, wielding those long curved unseemly looking nails some more.

"Auntie, I'm telling you the truth. We're not like that; we're friends, that's all" Daniel declared with the palm of his right hand facing his aunt as if he were about to take an oath. He added, " . . .we were in the Army together and since she's now stationed not too far from here, we decided to meet here and get caught up. Now, Aunt Sarah, what were you talking about . . . like we . . ."

"Boy sit yo little narrow tail down and lemme talk to you" Aunt Sarah ordered.

Javonica, who had been uncharacteristically quiet for a good portion of the unfolding of this drama, suddenly piped up with a guttural 'harrump, and an exaggerated roll of both her neck and her eyes.

"...'bout time somebody give him da' 4-1-1".

Aunt Sarah at once shot Javonica the silent curse, signaling her to be quiet. Before she pointed Daniel to the sofa, she pulled Patience into her arms and hugged her.

"Oh, baby, we been wait'in fa' you fa' a long time. I know God was gon' bring you home".

She stroked Patience's short brown hair that was beginning to show just a smidgen of gray, and for probably the first time in a long time, Daniel could see sincerity in his aunt's eyes. As if Aunt Sarah's actions were permission for her to hug Patience, too, Aunt Eva abruptly halted her circular march and did precisely that. She held Patience in her embrace for a long time and Daniel noticed the trembling of her shoulders, then saw the same in Patience. He knew then that they knew for sure.

"You look so much like yo mama, child . . . don't she Sarah?" Aunt Eva said between tears and a broad smile.

"Yeah, child. Jo was a pretty one . . . a fine young woman" Aunt Sarah confirmed, then, beckoned Patience onto the sofa just next to her.

"How y'all find one 'another?" Aunt Sarah asked, looking at Patience, who shrugged, but hadn't yet uttered a single word.

"We always had this'n . . ." Aunt Sarah said, with a thump to Daniel's arm, " . . . but we know you been out dey, baby. We know the God we serve would bring us all together . . . I'm just glad I live to see. I know yo' mama and yo' gran'mama dey shout'in in heaven right now, baby".

Aunt Eva nodded her agreement amidst her gleaming smile and the glistening tears that were still flooding her face.

"Yeah, we lost our baby sister way too young . . ." Aunt Eva stated, still nodding her head, and now rocking back and forth on the crowded sofa " . . . but He brung both'a Jo's chirn back to us! This is a blessed day, child".

Aunt Eva was again, overtaken with emotions as her shoulders shuddered with each convulsive sob. Daniel made room on the sofa and wrapped his aunt in a warm embrace. It was a few moments before he realized what Aunt Eva had said about 'both' of Jo's children'. When he looked up to confirm what he thought he'd heard, Patience's eyes were boring into his eyes relentlessly.

"Aunt Eva, didn't Aunt Josephine's son . . . mmhh . . . you know . . . didn't he . . . die?" Daniel struggled for words.

To Daniel's question, Patience uttered her first words in the last two or so hours.

"Yeah, Benjy's gone. . . so that leaves you and me".

Her words were so soft, so tranquil, as if she was halfway asleep or as if she was having a private conversation with herself. Daniel couldn't be sure she had said what he thought she did. He looked at her incredulously, as Patience got up from the sofa and dragged the nearby hassock to rest in front of Daniel's seat on the sofa. Patience sat on the brown leather foot rest with her knees touching one another, making her legs form an inverted 'V'. She reached her right hand out and gently, but deliberately loosened Daniel's left hand from around Aunt Eva's neck. She held his left hand in both of hers.

"Its just you and me; we're all that's left of Josephine".

Chapter 21

Even as he lay in his bed in Seattle, eight months and twenty-nine hundred miles away from the experience of that fateful Thursday, Daniel could still recall every single detail of that morning vividly. He could remember how many times his heart beat between his aunts' answers to his questions; he could remember precisely the number of times Patience's eyes blinked; he remembered how dry his throat felt; he could remember all the scents around him---each woman's cologne; the slight smell of mold in a house that had been closed up for seven months; he still remembered the strange taste of something bitter coming up the back of his throat. That's how profound that moment was; that's how unforgivable that information had been. Nearly eight eight months removed from that mild January day had done little to ease the magnitude of the betrayal he had felt.

One hundred and ninety-nine days had passed and Daniel still felt the exhaustion he'd felt that Thursday morning. He remembered throwing protocol to the wind when he forced the elderly and the uninvited from his parents' house. At that point it didn't matter to him what they thought of him; he wasn't even sure what he thought of himself. He just knew he had to be away from his trouble-making aunts and his trouble-making first cousin.

After a ruckus that included much crying, a lot of praying, some blasphemy, and the occasional physical nudging, Daniel was finally able to dispose of the blight that had infested his parents' home; the blight that had, by seven in the morning, contaminated his life and infused it with insanity. It was well after nine o'clock before he could get around to processing with Patience what had just transpired. Still dressed in the paradox of gaudy flannel pajamas wrapped with an obviously pricey and swank looking robe with the gold seal of some upscale hotel, Patience sat on the wood coffee table with her face in her hands. She was shaking her head from left to right.

"What in the world just happened? Who are those people? How did they know? How. . .?"

As if there was no abundance of available chairs in the living room, Daniel, placed the faux tiffany lamp on the floor and dragged one of his parents' end tables so that it was just in front of where Patience sat. He took a seat there, so that the two of them were sitting face-to-face, table-to-table, with their knees touching. He took Patience's left lower arm, so that she would be forced to look at him.

"Patience . . . I . . ."

Daniel stammered, cleared his throat and made a second attempt at answering Patience's questions. This time he looked piercingly, yet apologetically into her eyes.

"Patience, you know they're full of gossip and foolishness, right? That's just who they are; that's just what they do. You can't believe a thing they say! They're just trouble makers . . ."
Daniel shrugged his shoulders in exasperation, then, added as if for emphasis, " . . . just damn busy bodies! They've always been jealous of Mama . . . always been . . ."
Before Daniel could finish his last statement, Patience took her right hand and covered Daniels's hand that was holding her left arm. She looked up at him with apology in her eyes.
". . . but they're right this time, Daniel . . . they're not lying this time. Its true . . ."
She nodded slowly, then repeated her statement. This time her eyes floated in tears and every single one of her words was saturated with regret.
" . . . its true sweetie".
Daniel's brown eyes squinted and his pupils became pinpoint sharp. What had been warm and welcoming suddenly turned to daggers, poised to defend the honor of his identity.
"Patience, you don't know them! You don't know the kind of people they are, baby . . . they're full of game; they. . ."
Gripping her brother's hand even tighter, Patience slowly shook her head from left to right, and spoke with a bit more force both in her tone and in her inflection.
"Daniel! Daniel, I know you don't want to hear this, but . . . but its true; it really is! It's the truth. It was Josephine who gave birth to you; you're Josephine's child. We are Josephine's children".
For a few seconds Daniel was speechless. He couldn't believe it; he wouldn't believe it . . . because ". . . it wasn't true" he decided silently.
". . . who the hell was this crazy woman to come in here and tell me who my mama is?" he asked himself.

And even as angry as he was at Patience, Daniel knew he would not be rude to her; he would not say to her the things he was thinking. He less than gently removed Patience's hand from his and got up from his seat. He walked to the big picture window and looked out over the front yard, but never saw it; he never saw the rare cardinal in January that perched itself on the naked branch of the apple tree; he didn't see when the bright red bird flit over to a nearby oak.

"Do you know what you're saying? Patience do you even have a clue what you're saying?" he snapped without ever turning around to face her.

Patience did not respond to his questions. For what seemed like hours she sat while he stood---both in complete and utter silence. Although the birds had been singing earlier, they weren't any more; although they could both be certain that the refrigerator was still running, it, too, all of a sudden, was silent. The only sound in the house was the occasional tick of the mantel clock, and the soft chime as the long hand reached the quarter points of the hour.

Amidst the booming silence Daniel's mind replayed a conversation he had had with his mother in 1988. He remembered how his mother's reasons for not going to her sister's funeral had sounded lame and contrived; he thought about all Jessie had told him about their Aunt Josephine, and how his mother, just minutes later had either omitted what Jessie had told him or had minimized the significance of certain events. He remembered his confusion at his mother's blatant omission of her sister residing in a nursing home or of her sister's son's suicide; he recalled all the times he was not allowed to attend family gatherings. In that very instant Daniel came face to face with the reality that there were facts to which he had not been privy; that there were things going on in his family that his parents had not told him. While in this instant he had to acknowledge that there were things about his family that he didn't know, he held on to the belief that this was not one of them. His parents would never, he decided in his mind, have kept something like this from him.

Suddenly, Daniel felt like he had no more fight in him; he felt deflated---not because he thought less of his aunt; not because he wouldn't want to share DNA with someone of Patience's caliber, but because this was just too much; because all that he had heard . . . all that he had learned in less than twenty hours was just so far removed from what he knew. . . from what he believed. He wouldn't have a reason to doubt Patience, but what she was saying just couldn't be . . .his parents would never let him believe what was so blatantly untrue. At once he remembered Aunt Mary's admonition from the day before that he needed to hear the rest of the story.

"Was this the rest of the story?" he asked himself silently as the morning sun seared into his brown eyes. Daniel was deflated because, in listening to Aunt Sarah and Aunt Eva, and even to his first cousin, it seemed that everybody in his family knew who he was . . . everybody knew him . . . except him.

"How . . ." he wondered, " . . .had his classless cousins been privy to information about him that he, himself had never been allowed to know? How is it that his family had had such utter disrespect for him that people he considered not worthy of having his spit land on them were charged with having a key to his identity, when he, himself, wasn't allowed that same privilege?"

Both anger and confusion peppered with traces of disbelief laced every single one of Daniel's thoughts. With these and a host of other emotions kindling the fire in his heart, what floated to the forefront of Daniel's mind that bright Thursday morning was something akin to venomous. He wondered how his family members must have looked at him:

". . . poor, poor pitiful Daniel . . . not strong enough to handle the truth; not mature enough to handle his own truth; not man enough . . ." he thought mockingly.

As Daniel stood before the picture window with his back turned to Patience, she could see his anger from behind---she saw the crimson orb that his bald head had become.

He suddenly turned around with a jerk.

"I don't care what anybody says, Angeline Francis is my mama. She is my mama and Tan is my daddy and that's that!" He spat the words at Patience, then just as quickly turned back to peer out the window through the white sheer curtains. In what seemed like a nano-second he spun around to face Patience for the second time.

"C'mon. Get dressed" he ordered, and without question, Patience quietly obeyed.

Chapter 22

By noon Daniel's cell phone had been going off like crazy. Patience counted at least twenty–two attempted calls, herself. Daniel, however, would not respond to any of the callers. He didn't even check the caller ID not once. By this time he and Patience were sitting in the same chairs at the same table they had sat at less than twenty four hours earlier. Before they'd even gotten out of their car, Aunt Mary was already at the door with the storm door propped open, waiting for them.

"For once, son, they're not lying" Aunt Mary confirmed.

"So I'm not a Francis. . ." Daniel stated and asked in the same lackluster sentence.

Aunt Mary looked over to Patience as if to take a cue from the younger woman as to how she should proceed. Next she took Daniel's left hand into hers.

"You are a Francis" she said definitively.

"Hah!" Daniel perked up, now with even greater confusion written all across his face.

"You are a Francis" Aunt Mary re-stated, definitively.

"Aunt Mary . . .?" Daniel started, rubbing his head and face with his right hand.

"Son, this is a long and deep story, and God knows I never wanted you to find out like you did this morning. No, that was not the way for you to find out this stuff. Now I wish to God I had gone on and told you the whole thing yesterday. I wish your mama and daddy had'a told you about this before they passed. God knows they had time. I've been after Angeline to go on and tell you once you turned twenty–one, but any ways . . ." Aunt Mary agonized. She sighed a long deep sigh and continued.

"This is no way for you to find out, but it sure isn't fair either for other people to know all about your business and you don't even know yourself".

Aunt Mary paused again, with steep worry lines across her forehead. She shook her head and proceeded.

"God knows your daddy was a good man . . . a good provider, anyway. Angeline never wanted for a thing! All Tan expected from his wife was to obey his word, and stay home and take care of his house and his children. That was way more than any of us ever had or ever could expect . . . you know, son we come from hard times".

Daniel was committed to not showing any disrespect to Aunt Mary, but his patience was wearing thin with his aunt's lengthy prelude. He needed the old woman to get to the gist of the story.

"Tan wasn't perfect; no man is. Some men drink; some men beat their wives; some men spend their money in the street; and some men run around, ya' know".

Aunt Mary monitored Daniel's expressions closely, trying to read how he was handling what she was telling him. She waited for a response or a reaction. He gave her neither.

"That was just Tan's problem. He liked women" she said.

Aunt Mary had stopped talking as if that was the end of the story. The room was silent for at least three –to-four minutes. Daniel was processing what his aunt was saying, but somehow it felt like she was tossing words at his head; words that were hard as golf balls . . . and his head, in this analogy, was hard as a rock, so the golf ball words just couldn't seem to penetrate the hard shale against which they were being tossed. Nothing was sinking in, and at the same time, Daniel felt like he was in another orbit; a whole different realm; like he was floating in some netherworld where he didn't recognize anything around him.

"So Daddy cheated on Mama?" Daniel asked pointedly.

Aunt Mary nodded.

" . . .with Mama's own sister?" Daniel asked again, and again Aunt Mary nodded her head affirmatively.

Daniel leapt from his seat at the table, but realized he had nowhere to go . . . so he stood there.

"Aunt Mary . . .?" he started to ask, but she interrupted.

"I know . . . I know . . . child, I know this is a bitter pill to swallow . . . but your daddy loved you; good Lord, that man loved his son. . . Je--sus! He was happy to have a boy" Aunt Mary exclaimed, then added, ". . . your mama, too. She loved you no different than she loved your sisters. In fact she did everything in her power to protect you, Daniel".

With his left palm on his forehead and the butt of his right palm propping his body against the tiny wood table, Daniel shook his head in disbelief and uttered what sounded like a guttural grunt.

"Do my sisters know about this?"

"Oh, I doubt it, sweetie. Angeline kept them girls away from everybody in the family to make sure they didn't hear anything they weren't supposed to hear . . . anything that would shine your family in a light less than that of perfection; so, no! I doubt that they know. When you were born your oldest sister was probably old enough to suspect something, but I doubt that she would've had a reason to".

Daniel continued shaking his head.

"This is incredible! Absolutely incredible!" Daniel declared, then added, ". . . in twenty-four hours my whole world is turned up-side 'freak'in down!"

"Son, don't say that word" Aunt Mary warned pointedly, ". . . I understand that what you're hearing isn't the most pleasant news, but I'm still your elder, you hear".

"I said 'freak'in", Aunt Mary", Daniel defended.

"Yeah, but we know what you mean".

"I'm sorry, Aunt Mary, I didn't mean to be rude".

"Apologize to your sister, too" Aunt Mary ordered, pointing to her left.

Hearing Aunt Mary refer to Patience as his sister took Daniel aback. He realized that this was all so new; so unexpected; so . . . overwhelming

"Oh, God. I am so sorry, Patience . . . I didn't mean . . ." Daniel offered, but was interrupted.

"Daniel I didn't expect this to be easy . . . I just wanted us to connect . . . I needed us to connect . . . we're sister and brother and I wanted to honor that and I wanted you to know. I fully understand that this is going to be hard for you. I understand that what for me is a blessing---I finally find my family; my blood; my identity---might very well feel like a curse for you".

"Patience, you need to tell him the rest" Aunt Mary demanded.

"There's more?" Daniel asked incredulously.

"Son, I respect you as a man, so I'm going to make sure you have all the information I know. I'm not carrying any of this stuff with me to my grave. The less I carry, the lighter my burden so I can ascend into heaven. What you do with the information is your own business, but I'm going to give you the respect of putting the facts out there on the table" Aunt Mary declared passionately.

Before Aunt Mary had barely finished her preface of what was to come, Patience spoke up in a tone that suggested she, herself, was asking for Daniel's forgiveness.

"He's my father, too" she said softly.

Just like a top, Daniel spun his plump body around with the agility of an Olympics gymnast. His 360 degree turn ended with an abrupt and loudly uttered, "What!?"

"That's why the Tracey's were so mad at our mother, Daniel. She had cheated on her husband with her own sister's husband and had a baby. . . Josephine had boldly had affairs and, in at least two instances . . ."

Patience shrugged and diverted her eyes towards the gently swaying marsh grasses, before she continued.

". . . in at least two instances of infidelity, our mother had daringly slept with her own sister's husband . . . Tan Francis. . . . and she had Tan's children. . . you, first, then later, me. Although the Milledges did everything they could to cover for their sister, the Tracey's knew about you. When Ben Tracey came back from Korea his family was none too happy to let him know that his wife had given birth to her sister's husband's baby. Ben had a decision to make, and the one he made was not popular with his family. He had basically chosen his wife over his family. He had opted to stay married to Josephine. He loved her almost senselessly . . ."

As soon as Aunt Mary heard Patience's last sentence she felt compelled to confirm what her niece was saying.

". . . mmmmhhh hummmmm; you got that right, child. That man loved himself some Josephine. And no matter what she did, he would take her back . . .time and time again. Oh, he would beat the devil out of her, but he wasn't going to leave her. No, his family didn't like that one bit" Aunt Mary declared.

Patience absorbed her aunt's words and after a few seconds of quiet contemplation resumed telling her brother the story of how she learned about his maternity and her paternity.

". . . Ben, our mother's husband, decided that if Angeline could live with the fact of her husband and her sister having slept together, and that if Angeline had you as proof of that betrayal, then her burden was certainly much heavier than his. He decided that he loved his wife enough that he would get past it. When she got pregnant a second time and it turned out that that child---me---was likely another man's child, Josephine's husband had had it; he was tired of being the fool, and his family was there to remind him of just how his wife had mocked their marriage a hundred times over. Ben Tracey had heard the rumors, and he knew exactly who my father was, but when he divorced Josephine he took me with him. It was his sister who couldn't abide my presence after he died" Patience recapped.

"Well, what about Aunt Josephine's other son . . .? you know, the one . . . that . . .."? Daniel asked, searching desperately for words.

"Nobody talks about Benjamin, Jr." Patience said.

"Well, you know people don't like to talk about things like that, and since he's gone, nobody just don't say" Aunt Mary, said, closing the subject of Benjy's paternity.

"Has any of this been proven, or is this just speculation" Daniel asked.

"I met your parents just before the car accident, Daniel" Patience said before looking across the table at Aunt Mary.

"Son, I know you never met your daddy's family, but did he ever tell you anything about them?" Aunt Mary asked.

Daniel thought for a second before answering his aunt.

"His mama died in the forties, I remember him telling me that . . . and her name was . . . Oh my God! . . . so he knew about you . . . he knew Mama's sister . . . Oh, God! This is so crazy . . ." Daniel agonized.

"Its been proven, son, and your mama knew. Your daddy never denied that he fathered either of you, but if you're talking DNA testing, yes, all the mouth swab tests have been done and, well . . .we got all the paperwork and everything right in here" Aunt Mary said, pointing to her bedroom.

"I wanted the DNA tests just to be sure; just for my own peace of mind" Patience said.

". . . and Mama knew?" Daniel asked, again incredulously.

Both Aunt Mary and Patience nodded in unison, but neither said another word.

Chapter 23

"Several sessions back you asked me a pretty profound question, Daniel . . . a philosophical question. Do you remember?" Dr. Matthews asked.

"I think so" Daniel answered, then waited for the answer. When none came he sat up straight in his chair as if he was stunned by the extended silence.

"Well. . .?"

"Well, what?" the therapist asked.

". . . my question. . ." Daniel reminded her.

"I'm waiting for you to tell me, Daniel" Dr. Matthews said with a hint of a smirk flirting at the corners of her lips.

". . . ah I should've known" Daniel voiced, feigning disappointment.

". . . yes, you should have" Dr. Matthews bantered.

Daniel sprawled back onto the sofa with his legs spread apart and both feet planted firmly on the floor. His right arm was draped loosely over the back of the chair. Reese took note of how relaxed he appeared, both in posture and voice tone. She was pleased with Daniel's progress, but knew there were mountains yet to be climbed.

"I don't exactly know, Dr. Matthews" Daniel admitted nodding his head slowly. Dr. Matthews took note of what appeared to be some inconsistency in his gesture and his words.

"You're nodding affirmatively, Daniel, while you're verbalizing ambiguity. Help me understand that", she requested.

Daniel shrugged his shoulders while contorting his face in an exaggerated manner.

". . .don't know, ma'am. . . just don't know" he responded casually.

Then as if he was, himself, contemplating the incongruence of his behaviors and his word, Daniel got quiet and looked introspectively in front of himself, then started talking.

"I mean, all my life my parents made a clear distinction between us and some of my other relatives. They were 'them'. . ." Daniel said stretching his right arm out to indicate distance, " . . . and we were 'us'. There was nothing in between. They were the ones to not be around; they had no social status . . . they drank; they smoked ---cigarettes and other stuff, too---and they were of questionable moral character . . . they didn't work. We, on the other hand---our family and my mother's brother's family---we were 'good people'; we were the salt of the earth people---we went to church; we lived in a house, not in subsidized apartments; we went on vacations as a family; all six of my sisters went to college and that was never a question; all six of my sisters were married before they had any children, and that was also not a debatable issue. We were . . . well . . . we were middle class. They were less than us; they were less because they weren't middle class, and we were middle class because of my daddy. Unlike my mother's sisters' husbands and boyfriends, my daddy took care of his family. He was what a man was supposed to be and did what a man was supposed to do. We were the perfect American family---intact and picture perfect, with one daddy, one mama, and no dangling threads".

". . .dangling threads . . .? Reese asked.

". . . dangling threads . . . you know . . . no outside children. All my mother's children were fathered by her one and only husband, and all my father's children were by my mother . . . no dangling threads" Daniel clarified.

". . . and you spent a good deal of time with the very cousins and aunts that your mother didn't want you around?" Dr. Matthews asked.

"I was just being defiant. I was being a teenager, and truth be told, being around them always assured me that I was better than somebody" Daniel acknowledged.

"You mentioned something like this early in our meetings. Was it the same kind of assurance you got when Patience became your project?" Dr. Matthews asked, using air quotes at the word project.

"You know what Doc? I don't remember saying or even suggesting that, but I'm not going to deny it. In fact, now that you've said it, I need to go on and own it. Yeah. Yeah, that's exactly what it was . . . and you know, now that I think about it, that's probably why I was so nervous about meeting her in Bristol Creek this past January. I didn't know what our relationship would be without me being the top dog, so to speak. Now that she had outranked me, I wondered if she would feel about me like I felt about her back then" Daniel admitted.

Reese nodded her understanding but did not speak.

". . . and you know what . . ." Daniel went on, " . . . that isn't a good feeling. That's why I was so nervous, 'cause I knew that feeling; I *know* that feeling! That's what I felt the whole time I was married to Vickie. I knew I was less than; I could never measure up to their standards . . . no matter what. I was her project".

After about a minute of silence Dr. Matthews asked: "Was that the first time---when you were married to Vickie---that you'd ever felt inadequate?"

Daniel stilled his gesturing right arm and leaned forward into that protective position Reese had observed him assuming whenever he was forced to confront an issue that challenged his emotions. He leaned forward with his elbows resting on his knees and his hands making a tent. Before answering the therapist's question, Daniel's two index fingers touched at the tip and did a dance in front of his lips. He exhaled long and audibly, then spoke.

"No. No, that was not my first rodeo, Doc".

The silence served as Daniel's signal to go on.

"I had no responsibility growing up; what ever I wanted was pretty much given to me. The only way my parents knew I was alive was when I got in trouble drinking or when I defied them and hung out at Aunt Sarah's or Aunt Ruby's. They weren't neglectful or anything like that. I never did anything so I never learned to do anything; I never became proficient at anything. No matter what I screwed up, somebody would pick up the tab: Mama and Daddy, or one of my sisters. Hell, if things got bad enough I had no doubt that one of my aunts or even my uncle would come to my rescue. I never learned how to master anything because I never had to".

"Is that strange, Doc?" Daniel asked after a few moments of silence.

"Do *you* think it's strange?" the counselor asked.

Daniel shrugged, then answered.

"Yeah. Yeah its strange alright".

"Is it?" Dr. Matthews challenged gently.

"Yeah it's strange, but at the same time it makes sense . . . I mean. . . that I gravitate toward people who I deem to be less than me. I know all about . . . uummh, . . . dang . . . I'm try'in to remember that theory about when you want to reach your highest potential . . . you know what I'm talk'in about?" Daniel asked, snapping his finger in frustration.

By now Daniel was on his feet and he was pacing back and forth the full length of the office.

". . . self actualization . . .?" Dr. Matthews ventured.

"That's it! That's the word. I knew you would know . . . I took a few psych courses when I was working on my degree" Daniel revealed with a smile that quickly faded.

Dr. Matthews nodded her head in understanding.

". . . another failure . . ." Daniel said, then added, ". . .didn't finish that either".

"Let's get back to your self actualization, Daniel". Dr. Matthews' redirection, prompted Daniel to return to his story.

"Okay, here's what I think . . . and this is only my interpretation of what I've been doing . . . probably ever since childhood: everybody wants to be at the top of their game; everybody wants to know that there is something they excel at. . . be the big man or the top dog at least sometimes. I couldn't be that at home, well because . . . just because. Because I was the baby . . . the one everybody looked after. Everybody took care of me---my sisters; my mama; my daddy. I never took care of anybody . . . not even myself. When I was hanging out over at Aunt Ruby's, heck I was better off than any of them just because of not having to live in public housing, if nothing else. So that alone put me out front. . . ahead of them. . . better than them. Plus when I was there nobody was look'in out for me, necessarily. It was every man for himself and God for us all over there" Daniel quipped. "Being over there with them was my only opportunity to prove to myself that I could do anything; at least over there I had to learn to look out for myself.

Daniel stopped walking just as he stopped talking. He turned to his left and looked his counselor square in the eyes.

"Is any of this making any sense to you, Dr. Matthews?"

"It is. Is it making sense to you?" she rebounded.

"Yeah. It is. This is like some type of epiphany. It's all coming together and it explains so much. . ." Daniel said. Daniel had stopped pacing for a few seconds, eyeing the counselor to assess whether or not she was understanding the depth of his sudden insights, but now resumed his stride.

"So, I seek out people and situations that I believe are below me or less than me so their circumstances, if nothing else, affirms my status, and then my worth. Is that what you're saying, Dr. Matthews?" Daniel asked.

"Is that what *you're* saying, Daniel?"

"That's exactly what I'm saying, Doc. That's exactly what I'm saying. I'm saying I have a self esteem problem and I need to stop using other people to define my worth in this world. . . . and you know what...?"

The obviously rhetorical question didn't wait for an answer as Daniel proceeded with his analysis.

". . . when I married Sheila's mother I don't know that I loved her . . .not as much as I admired her; I admired her status, plus my parents were happy with her status, too.   I believe she might have loved me, but I'm certain I turned out to be a big disappointment for her. At the same time, though I wanted her family to define me . . . define my value as worthy of being among the Elsey's. Being embraced by a family of that stature would surely confirm my status. So, instead of trying to build our own life together as a viable family, I wasted at least four years trying to be an Elsey, and shivering in my boots all along. When I failed at rising to the standard of being an Elsey, I high tailed it straight to the other end of the spectrum---to Aisha. She didn't have anything and didn't want anything, so I became her hero; her savior; her knight in shining armor. Anyway you look at it, I was better than my second wife. Instead of trying to measure up to the Elsey's, I was now the top dog; I was the standard setter. If nothing else, I knew for sure that I was better than my second wife. I knew it from the day I met her and to be honest with you, Dr. Matthews, I rejoiced in that fact on my wedding day. It felt so good to be on top; to not be looked at as less than. . . as inadequate. . . as not ever being able to measure up. Truth be told, that's what attracted me to Aisha. I had everything she didn't---a career; economic security; and the right background".

Daniel sighed heavily, then continued, ". . . she needed me. For the first time in my life, somebody actually needed me. I took Aisha out of the projects and made her as close to a lady as is possible for someone so coarse and lacking even a semblance of culture".

Daniel shuddered and made a guttural sound that mimicked a horse's whinny. He looked around the room with a sadness in his eyes, then continued sharing with the counselor the insights that both client and counselor knew were signs of his growth.

". . . that's why I married her. . . " Daniel confessed.

As he sat with his legs crossed widely, Daniel laced his two hands together and cupped them over his mouth as if he needed to filter words that might escape.

" . . . I married her . . . because I thought I was better than her . . . better than her whole family. . . better than the very children I fathered with her. . ." he added with his voice trailing off.

"I suppose I'm a real piece of work, aren't I?" Daniel asked.

Dr. Matthews shrugged her shoulders and raised her eyebrows questioningly. She smiled at Daniel's quirky but insightful interpretations of his life experiences, but more so at his fluidity of movement, thought and emotion. She noted that he was lithe in his stride as he allowed his thoughts to flow without constraint. She noticed how he dared to assign responsibility to himself for his behaviors and, more importantly for his thoughts even when they were not necessarily flattering or when they were just plain selfish.

Daniel returned to his seat almost as unceremoniously as he had risen in the first place. He breathed what could have been a sigh of relief or a sigh of exhaustion---it would not have been easy to surmise which it was at this point. Either way, there was a look of tranquility about his face. He had reached a resolve, it seemed, and the counselor suspected that he would, in his own time and in his own way, allow her access to that place of reconciliation.

After more than four minutes of ear splitting silence, Daniel rose from his chair. He ran his hands deep into his pockets, then stretched his entire body as long as his five feet nine inches would allow, lifting himself up on his toes.

"Wow! I never thought I could or would say those words . . . never thought I could speak my true motives . . .I feel hopeful, Doc. I feel that if I can be completely honest with myself . . . and you, too. . . then I can do something about me".

Part III---

. . . that to which we return

"At the time appointed he shall return,
and come toward the south;
but it shall not be as the former . . .
(Dn. 11: 29)

Chapter 24

"Of course I'll be there, Daniel. I'm insulted that you believe you need to invite me. She's my aunt, too" Patience lamented.

"I know. I'm sorry, babe" Daniel apologized.

". . . but thanks for letting me know. I've visited her a few times since we were there in January, and we had established quite a bond. Since she had no children, who's in charge?" Patience asked.

"Her next of kin would be Aunt Sarah and Aunt Eva, I suppose . . . but then it could be Uncle Jessie, but somehow I doubt that" Daniel admitted.

". . . because . . .?" Patience asked.

"Well, he's a man with his own family, so I imagine Aunt Mary would have left her sisters in charge of her affairs" Daniel surmised.

"I've never met him . . . Uncle Jessie, I mean, but have spoken to him on the phone while visiting Aunt Mary. I've been in contact with Aunt Sarah and Aunt Eva, but only on a cursory level . . . I remembered that morning this past January; and I remembered your warnings, so I've kept a safe distance from them" Patience informed.

" . . .cursory . . .? Daniel inquired

"Yeah, you know, like to wish them happy mother's day or on holidays. I've got their birthdays written down, so I've sent cards and flowers for those occasions . . ." Patience explained.

"Since they all know how to get in contact with me . . . I mean they even saw me at the hospital less than seventy –two hours ago, I'm surprised no one has called me to say that Aunt Mary passed. Thank you, Daniel for considering me a member of the family" Patience said with a tinge of sorrow and regret in her words.

"I'm headed that way first thing in the morning. Why don't you stay at Mama and Daddy's with me . . ."

Realizing the insensitivity of his words, Daniel flinched, then offered a feeble correction.

" . . . you know what I mean . . . you . . ."

"I understand, Daniel . . . and the fact of the matter is, they are your parents; that's your *mama* and your daddy" Patience said matter-of-factly.

After a few seconds of silence, Patience exhaled long and hard. Daniel could hear the exhaustion in her sigh. He, for the first time since January, considered how exhausted she must be. He knew how worn out he had been just since his first word of all the scandals, lies, and betrayals going on right under his nose. He realized, finally, that this all must have been completely overwhelming for Patience. For the first time he gave serious consideration to how he might be feeling were he in her shoes.

He concluded that he very probably would have abandoned this search a long time back. He doubted that he would have been able to stomach that the roots from which he sprung would or could have been so infested with pathology.

"I don't know, Daniel. I felt like I was embraced with Aunt Mary. With the way this has gone down, I'm not so sure . . ."

Before Patience could get to the gist of what she wanted to convey, Daniel interrupted fervently.

"What do you mean you don't know? Patience this is going to take some time . . . and yeah, I don't blame you for feeling some type of way about them not calling you, but *I'm* calling you. *I'm* your brother. Yeah, I'm disappointed that you weren't included among the first to get a call, but I'm your brother; maybe it's my place to let you know, after all."

Without the benefit of a preface, or of even being sure that Patience was okay with the issue of feeling like she'd been treated like an outsider, Daniel abruptly changed the subject.

"Listen, if you stay at a hotel you'll be even that much more removed from the family. Come on over to the house" Daniel insisted.

"Aren't your sisters coming? They're not staying at your parents'?" Patience asked, looking for an excuse to distance herself from a situation that was becoming increasingly uncomfortable. She was feeling very alone since the death of the last person with whom she felt a safe familial bond. Patience admitted to herself that although Daniel was her ally, she didn't know that he commanded the kind of respect Aunt Mary did; she wasn't sure if he could carry his weight and hers, too, when it came to his family members. Although she could easily go head to head with any of them that wanted to go a round or two, she believed any confrontation with the Milledges or any of their descendants would create discord between she and Daniel and then between Daniel and his family.

"No, they and their highfalutin husbands are going to breeze in and out of here like Aunt Mary's funeral is an afternoon tea party. Only Jessie, Jackie, and Millicent are coming and they're all staying at hotels in town. This house isn't big enough for them anymore" Daniel lamented.

"Have you told them, Daniel?" Patience asked.

"Just Jess" Daniel answered briefly and evasively.

After the sixty-seven seconds of ear-splitting silence, Daniel exhaled and brought himself to the part of the conversation he had dreaded having with Patience.

"Patience, they're not hearing this. I know them. Jess is the only one that's even close to reality, and even she is a bit tentative. But Millicent, Jackie, Angie, Erica and Nina are off the chart with this whole thing. They don't want to let go of the façade of a life we had; they can't get pass the idea that Mama and Daddy had all these secrets; that our family was no better than the very people our parents looked down their noses at. It pains them, Patience, to think, even for a second, that our family is even lower on the moral scale than the kinds of people you would see on a Jerry Springer show. In fact, Angie and Nina are so much older than me, I don't really feel like I know them well enough to have an adult conversation with them".

As she heard her brother's last sentence, Patience believed her assessment of Daniel within his family was on target. This frightened her more than anything. The very person who she believed could hold her back couldn't even hold his own . . . not with his family members, anyway. Patience groaned.

". . . an adult conversation? What does that mean? You just turned forty-three and your sisters still don't accord you the respect of being a man?" she probed disbelievingly.

"Listen, just come on to the house; we'll talk about this when you get to Bristol Creek, okay? Safe travels, kiddo" Daniel said as he ended the call without answering any of Patience's questions or addressing her concerns.

The four hour flight through three time zones and the long layover in Atlanta flew by like one of the old Super Sonic Transports. Daniel realized that it would take far more than the nine hours it took for him to get from Seattle to Charleston to make some sense of what he needed to do to become an adult in his family. He had been able to reconcile the need for this change through therapy. He had even been able to put the notion in words so eloquent he might have made Wadsworth proud, but now that the rubber was meeting the road, he had to admit that he was stumped. He had become quite comfortable with the way things were; with everybody treating him like a little boy; and with himself being a pseudo-adult. It took the events of the last few months to bring him face to-face with his need to move beyond the deceptive comfort of hypocrisy. He had finally, at the very gates of his forty-third year, come to grips with the fact that that pillow of disingenuousness on which he had rested his head was not only anachronous, it was just plain irresponsible. It, he had come to know, was what had stunted his growth and was precisely what continued to stunt his growth. The deception of ease had lulled him into a dangerous kind of complacency, where nothing was his problem, and whatever was, could and would be solved by someone else.

As he leaned against the window of the 'A' seat on the airplane that was the final leg of his flight, Daniel thought about his eldest son. He admitted, for the first time in twenty years that he had been a sorry excuse for a father. He basically had abandoned Blade. He recalled that when Carla announced that she was pregnant that he was beside himself with anger.

As the puddle-hopper plane made the bumpy taxi down the runway, Daniel acknowledged for the first time to himself how he had left Carla out in the cold. He had allowed his sisters and his parents to take the lead in fighting her when all the mother of his child had reasonably expected from him was that he take care of his son. He remembered also how they gladly took up his fight---reminding him that Carla wasn't the kind of girl he should have gotten involved with in the first place; calling her ugly names; telling him he needed to get far, far away from her. And so that is precisely what he did. He walked away from Carla and walked away from his own flesh and blood. The story, he reminded himself, was not that different with Aisha either. Again, his family had decided for him that these kinds of people weren't good for him, so he quietly walked away from two more children. He had been convinced that as long as he sent a check every month, he had done his duty.

Daniel wondered if he could turn things around at this late date; could he reasonably expect that he could or should step back into his children's lives and make an attempt at salvaging these relationships. Even as he considered these strategies, he imagined the fight he would get from his sisters.

Almost immediately, he shook his head as if awaking from a bad dream.

"That's the problem . . ." he said out loud before he realized he was still on the airplane. When the passenger in the center seat looked at him askance, Daniel realized that he was talking out loud to himself. He realized that he probably appeared to the woman to be some kind of nut case. He went back to his thoughts, but made a conscious effort to contain his thoughts within his mind.

". . . that's exactly the problem. . ." he resumed his discussion with himself, ". . . I've included them in all my business; I've spent my life asking everybody's permission instead of stepping out on my own and making decisions, then dealing with the consequences".

Chapter 25

"For people that's supposed to be so sophisticated and supposed to be such Christians, I gotta' tell y'all, right now y'all are not acting like either one" Daniel declared without apology.

As Millicent wobbled her way to the back of the dining room for her fourth Long Island iced tea, she refuted her brother's assessment of her and her sister's behaviors. "Listen baby brother . . ." Millicent started in on yet another round of attacks she and Jackie had launched against Daniel's relationship with Patience Bright.

Daniel scowled as if he was in physical pain. He had always hated being referred to as 'baby brother' by either of his sisters. While he could abide the pet name when Jessica used it, he was assured that when either Millicent, or Angie, and especially Nina used it, the purpose was to remind him of his place in the family---that of a baby; someone with no voice and no ability to look out for even his most basic needs. Whenever he had asked his sisters to stop referring to him as 'baby brother' none of them except Jessica had honored his request. And here he was, he thought, just turning the page toward his mid forties, and his sisters refused to see him as anything other than a baby; someone who needed help managing his life. As he heard what he had come to see as a condescending pet name, the ire that was slowly rising in the back of his throat suddenly picked up its pace. Bitter bile was now pulsing through every vein in his body and it was taking every ounce of resolve on his part not to raise his voice at his sister. Daniel had resolved within the last few years that he would seek out more mature ways of conveying his feelings. He had come to understand all too keenly that yelling and screaming obscenities and calling people ugly names and using insulting words would always come back to haunt him in the end. He knew also that whenever he behaved that way it was an indication of his own immaturity and that these behaviors garnered so much less respect than had he approached his confrontations with greater tact and diplomacy. The blood that had heated and colored his neck a bright crimson was abating as he reminded himself of his therapist's mantra that he could never demand respect, but rather could command it based on how he managed challenging situations. He had decided in his last session with Dr. Matthews that he was committed to doing precisely that--- commanding the respect of his family by changing his behaviors to be reflective of his growth.

". . . you need to stop being so gullible. All your life we had to look out for you; bail you out of this thing or the next. Mama and Daddy and all of us done save your behind about a thousand times . . ." Millicent continued. By this time Jackie had chimed in with a litany of Daniel's ill-advised relationships and the children he had fathered as a result of those relationships.

" . . . oh, Lord, and that ghetto queen he hooked up with!" she guffawed and added, " . . . you sure know how to pick'em, Junie. You need to understand that there are some people you just gotta stay away from. . . now you got all them little ghetto children . . ." Jackie snickered.

Daniel kept repeating to himself that he was not going to do what his family expected him to do; he was not going to succumb to their taunting and have a temper tantrum. He admitted in that moment however, that trying not to shout was a monumental task. That, after all, was what he knew; that was what they expected; and that, they all knew, would keep them in their role of rescuing their poor hapless baby brother from his poor hapless self. The thought of this spiraling cycle of emotional sickness made Daniel feel physically ill. While two of his sisters continued with their long list of their brother's broken relationships and dependence on them to correct his misdeeds, Daniel sat quietly at the table with is right elbow resting in the thick solid wood surface on which all three of them had eaten a lifetime of meals.

To abate his hurt and anger, Daniel tuned out both Jackie and Millicent and focused on the charge before him. He gently squeezed the bridge of his nose, as he exhaled slowly and deliberately. His head turned to the right to see Jessie's disdain for her sisters. It was when he heard her voice attempting to intervene on his behalf that he placed his right hand on top of her left to quiet her. At this point he stood up and placed both his palms flat against the surface of the table. In a slightly stooped over posture Daniel looked around the table at all three of his sisters, each one in her own turn. All at once quiet pervaded the room, and with teeth clenched tightly as if this were a mechanism to tame his words, Daniel made an unyielding declaration of his expectations regarding Patience.

"The three of you are my sisters and I love each of you. I have always been committed to not saying or doing anything to hurt you. This has always been my rule of how to treat you as sisters and I won't change that now; I won't change that even in the face of my disappointment or my anger. That simply won't happen. I've got to acknowledge to you that I've not always treated other people that way, though. I've had this ridiculous notion in my head that if I treat the other women I love well, that somehow that would be a betrayal to my sisters or my mother. . ."

Millicent interrupted with " . . . some a' them women you had were not worthy of good treatment".

"Millicent, please don't interrupt me" Daniel requested quietly. In the presence of three slack-jawed women, Daniel continued.

"If she was with me, she was worthy of my respect. I'm not saying that you had to love or even respect them, but I should have. You see Millicent, if I don't respect them, and I'm with them . . . laying with them. . . then, that only says that I have no regard for myself. Now, I've allowed my family members to speak ill of my wives, my girlfriends, and even my children".

Daniel exhaled, then turned his face up to the ceiling in a effort to avert the tears that were threatening the threshold of his eyelids. He composed himself in a few seconds and walked over to the archway that connected the dining room and kitchen. He propped his back against the load bearing joist and continued.

"That stops today. That stops now . . . right now. Do I make myself clear?"

The stunned looks on the faces of the three women indicated that this discussion or this kind of discussion was not something they had ever heard or expected from their brother. There was an eerie calm to Daniels voice, along with a slow and deliberate flow of his words that conveyed to Jackie, Jessie, and Millicent that their brother's utterances were not the product of anger.

"That stops this instant . . ." Daniel reiterated, then continued.

"I can't tell you how to feel about Aisha or Vickie. I can't tell you how to feel about Blade, Sheila, Frisco, Sienna, and Parker. I can't tell you how to feel about Carla . . ."

Millicent interrupted with guttural ". . .harrumph!".

"Millicent . . ." Daniel said in the tone of a warning before he resumed expressing his dismay with their attacks.

"I can't stop you from saying negative things about any of these people, including Holly, or Patience . . . but what I will tell you is that I will no longer entertain a discussion with either of you or any of my other sisters about my ex-wives, my baby mama's or my children. No matter how I feel about any of these people or how our relationships went, at some time in my life each of these women have meant something to me. Some have meant enough to me that I shared my bed with them. All except one has given me the gift of my blood. . . my children, and I simply will not take part in any bashing of any of them. Am I clear?" Daniel asked.

In silence, all three sisters nodded affirmatively.

"Now . . ." Daniel proceeded, walking to the oven to check the status of the chicken he was roasting for that night's dinner.

". . . about Patience . . ." he continued, closing the oven and returning to his place against the vertical beam that framed the pass-through.

"Patience is my sister . . . and if either one of you has a problem with that, then, that is your problem, not mine. Whatever Daddy did is what he did. It's not my place or yours to think we can pass judgment on him . . . and you don't need to question how this all impacted Mama or their marriage, either. Mama made the decisions she did and so it was. None of us . . . not a single one of us. . . can indict them for how they chose to handle their lives or their marriage" Daniel stated emphatically but calmly. He looked around the table in an effort to gauge his sisters' reactions, then continued.

". . . and like all my other six sisters, I love Patience and will treat her with the same respect I have accorded you. I will not entertain any discussion of, or participate in any bashing of her either".

After a few seconds of quiet Millicent asked, " . . .so what do you suppose she wants?"

Before the last word of Millicent's question had barely crossed her lips the first six bars of Amazing Grace chimed from the great big oak front door.

"Good question, Millicent, and perfect timing, too. You can get the answer straight from the horse's mouth" Daniel stated with a broad smile on his face.

By the time Daniel swung open the door to his deceased parents' living room all three of the Francis children who had come home for their aunt's funeral had scrambled from their chairs to see the women who at least two of them had decided was a fraud or a scam artist. Even as Daniel reached across the door jamb to wrap the Sergeant Major in a brotherly embrace, Jessie had shoved him aside and was herself, in a welcoming caress with Patience. Daniel noted that the hug was an extended one before he noticed the shudder of both women's shoulders.

". . . ah shucks, y'all; no more cry'in, please" Daniel drawled in jest.

Although Millicent and Jackie never crossed the door sill, Patience was accosted with their hugs and warm welcome, too. Daniel peered at the four women with a confused look on his face.

"Did we just now get into a near knock-down drag-out over the issue of Patience staying here?" he asked himself. He didn't say this out loud, but Jackie, Millicent and Jessie knew exactly what their brother was thinking. While Jessie had tried hard to support her brother's enthusiasm about Patience Bright, she couldn't be sure. . . couldn't be certain that she could trust her brother's judgment about the story that sounded too bizarre. Millicent and Jackie, however, had been adamant that Daniel had fallen prey to a scam. Even after checking out Patience's paternity and Daniel's maternity with Aunt Mary before she was too ill to tell what she knew, neither Millicent nor Jackie was willing to believe it. Both women had held out hope that the story of their own lives, and hence the family from which they sprung, was pristine and without flaw. To have readily owned the flaw in their family, they thought, would make their current worlds a farce.

On the eve of the funeral of their aunt, five of Tan Francis' eight children broke bread at their father's dining room table. With the table cleared save for dessert and a bottle of cabernet sauvignon, Daniel playfully poked at Jackie under the table, then reminded Millicent of an inquiry she needed to make.

" . . . oh, Patience, Millicent has a question she wants to ask you".

As Jackie, Jessie and Daniel roared with laughter, Millicent's jaw dropped in embarrassment. Patience merely looked on, confused.

Jackie came to her sister's rescue.

"I'm sorry, Patience, Daniel's being a jar head tonight . . . you have to know we had the conversation about you. . ." Jackie said, using air quotes to emphasize the word 'the'.

Before Jackie could finish her sentence, Patience picked up the thought with a good natured smile on her face.

". . . and of course, you were trying to figure out what it is I wanted, right? . . ." Patience asked, then continued. "That just makes sense. I'm a stranger stepping into your world, and it's reasonable for you to think that I might have ulterior motives".

". . . I never thought for a second . . ." Daniel started with a shrug before Patience challenged him.

". . . come now, Daniel" she said with a sly smile. "You were not happy for a while. . ." she reminded.

"Well listen, kid . . . you rocked my world! I mean this whole thing has been life changing. With this kind of information I had to rethink everything I thought I knew about me; which means I had to rethink me; who I am; what I stand for; where I need to go from here . . ." Daniel explained.

"Listen to him calling her 'kid'! Patience he's so happy to have a little sister it isn't even funny" Jackie noted.

"Yeah, I know . . ." Patience acknowledged, then added, " . . . and I know I rocked your world. I didn't mean to scare you, but if I was going to do anything with this information I had to do it before Aunt Mary was no longer with us. She had the information that put all the pieces of this puzzle together.

"Who would'a' thunk!?" Millicent chimed in, shaking her head from side to side. At the phrase, they all laughed heartily.

"Phew . . . yeah, imagine the kinds of secrets families are hiding every day" Daniel said, still shaking his head from left to right in wonderment.

"Man, I had to go to therapy for a while" Daniel said.

At Daniel's admission of seeking counseling, Jackie literally dropped the utensil she was using to scoop butter pecan ice cream out of the quart sized Hagen Daaz carton.

"What?!" she asked, both amazed and amused.

"What are you so ga-ga about? I can't go to counseling?" Daniel asked.

"Junie, I just can't imagine you in counseling" Jackie almost screamed. "Did it help?"

"Hell yeah, it helped! I'm sane aren't I?" Daniel retorted.

"Well, now, Daniel . . . the question of your . . ."Millicent started jokingly, before Daniel intercepted her tease.

"Hey . . . hey! Give me a break, ladies. Listen, I got one boulder after another, after another dropped on me in short order: in less than twenty-four hours I learn I got a sister that was my mentee twenty years ago; then I learn that my mama ain't really my mama, but rather, my aunt, who I never met, is really my mama, and that my daddy is my daddy 'cause he cheated on my mama with my mama's sister . . . man that's some deep stuff . . . I mean some really deep stuff. . .that's the kinda' stuff to make a man jump off a bridge or something".

"You ain't ly'in" Millicent confirmed.

Patience smiled and offered her apology for how overwhelming the process had to have been for Daniel.

"I appreciate all of you embracing me as you have. Thank you" Patience added.

". . . now lets tell the truth . . ." Daniel spurred, but was not allowed to finish before Jessie interrupted.

" . . . yeah, but the second I saw her I knew . . . I saw it, and I felt it".

"Felt what?" Daniel asked with the look of cluelessness written across of forehead. To her brother's absentmindedness, Jessica thumped the left side of his head.

"ouch!" Daniel yelled, feigning hurt.

"You met her twenty two years ago! You couldn't tell?" Jessica asked.

"Tell what?" Daniel continued, still in a fog.

"Oh my God, Junie! Look at Patience. Look at her. When you opened that door tonight I saw Mama standing there. Patience looks more like mama than any of us" Jackie declared.

". . . and I can remember Aunt Jo. She was a younger version of Mama. I see her all over you, Patience", Millicent stated.

". . . and you can *feel* it . . . the connection . . ." Jessie said with a shudder.

"You know I can remember sometimes I caught myself staring at Patience because I thought she looked familiar. And of course Vickie insisted up and down that we looked alike, but it wasn't until we were here in January, that I remember being stunned by how much she looks like Mama . . . remember that Patience?" Daniel noted.

Patience nodded confirmation of Daniel's observations of the likeness between herself and her aunt Angeline.

" . . . until Aunt Mary told us about Patience being Aunt Josephine's child, I just thought making her look like mama was a part of my grief process. But once Aunt Mary told me who her mama was it just made sense" Daniel explained.

Chapter 26

It was close to sun-up by the time Patience made it to a bedroom and crashed her exhausted body against the cool white bed linen. She inhaled the light floral scent of what was likely the fabric softener someone had used in the laundry. Although each of the Francis women had booked rooms at a local hotel, they all opted in the end to sleep at their parents' house on Wednesday night. Jessie and Millicent had claimed their parents' bedroom, while Daniel took his old childhood sleeping quarters.   Jackie took a third bedroom, leaving Patience with the fourth one.

"I thought y'all highfalutin little wenches were gonna stay in your expensive hotel rooms" Daniel commented jokingly.

"Oh hush, Junie . . ." Jackie said as she yawned unapologetically.

" . . . and leave all this fun; you must done gone and lost your mind, Daniel Tanner Francis, II" Millicent chirped.

"That's Daniel Tanner Francis, *Jr*." Daniel corrected in jest.

"Y'all were gonna stay at a hotel?" Patience asked with her brows furrowed.

"This is the first time we've been to the house since . . . since . . . the accident. I wasn't sure if . . . you know . . ." Jessie grappled for the words.

"I see" Patience offered.

"No, you don't see . . ." Daniel called his sisters out. "These heifers always stay at a hotel when they come to town" he noted.

". . .yeah. . . you're right, June. Usually when we come to town our families are with us, Patience . . . you know like for family reunions, weddings, stuff like that. This is the first time either of us have been in Bristol Creek without our husbands or our children, so I suppose old baldy over there is right . . ." Jessie joked.

After a few minutes of silence, each member departed the table one by one, with Jessie and Patience being the last two. Patience appreciated the time this gave her to talk with Jessie one on one. She had felt a connection with Jessie immediately, plus she already knew that Jessie was her brother's favorite sister.

" . . . so you're a Major in the Army?" Jessie inquired.

Patience laughed and corrected her half sister.

"No, I'm a Sergeant Major. It's an enlisted rank, whereas a Major is an officer's rank".

"Oooh. . . but your rank is pretty up there, right?"

"It's an E-9; it's the highest enlisted rank there is" Patience clarified.

". . . so, then, you got it go'in on" Jessie asked and stated in the same sentence.

Patience laughed again, then shook her head from side to side. She looked Jessie dead in the eyes, lifted her left eyebrow and confirmed Jessie's assessment.

"I'm not sure what 'got it go'in on' looks like, but I suppose you can say I *got* it go'in on. Professionally I'm at a really good place, if that's what you mean. I'm preparing to retire in the next four –to- five years, and then I'll teach".

"I am impressed. You've got it all planned out, Patience. I, on the other hand, am just winging it".

"Sometimes that's what we have to do, Jessie; sometimes we have to wing it until we can find our footing".

"Was finding your family a part of finding your footing?" Jess asked almost solemnly.

Patience took on a contemplative look, with her eyes focused, yet, looking at nothing in particular. She nodded slowly, then twisted her head to her right to face Jessie.

"You know what, I hadn't thought of it in those terms . . . but you're probably right".

Patience thought for a few more seconds then shook her head more vigorously and more definitively.

"You *are* right; you're very right. This was the missing piece of my life. The not knowing left me always longing, always wanting, but at the same time, I was afraid to pursue the knowledge . . ." Before Patience could finish her statement, Jessie interrupted with what appeared to be a naïve question.

"Afraid of what?" she said looking quizzically at Patience.

Patience turned her whole body the ninety or so degrees it took to position her face to face with Jessie.

". . . afraid of what. . .!?" she asked, sounding astounded.

"yeah . . ." Jessie persisted, ". . . what would there be to be afraid of?"

"Afraid of this, Jessie!" Patience said without realizing she had raised her voice an octave above what was normal conversational tone.

The blank look on Jessie's face cued Patience that the woman seated at the table with her really didn't have a clue about what this process must have been like for Patience. She realized in that instant that although they shared a common blood, their lives were as far apart as the two poles of the earth. In the past the soldier in Patience would have found Jessie's brand of naivete nauseating; her tolerance for that level of vulnerability was grossly inconsistent with the vigilance she had needed to have advanced her career to its current level, and it was certainly inconsistent with the skills she had needed to survive growing up in the foster care system. In the past she would have resented that a woman who shared the same blood as she did had been accorded the privilege of frivolity it would take for an adult to be so virginal in her thinking. On this night, though, Patience realized that she had grown way past those inconsequential feelings. She had learned over the course of her life, and especially within the past several years of leaning on Aunt Mary, that forgiveness and love had erased all the antagonism she had once felt.

With this in the back of her mind, Patience proceeded to explain her apprehensions about locating her family to the sister who was only about six years older than her, yet decades younger than her in wisdom. With that Patience adjusted her tone to accommodate both the sleeping and the dreaming.

"Jessie, do you know what it's like to put your credibility on the line? . . .to be subject to scrutiny as if you have committed a crime or hurt someone? . . . to have people automatically assume the worst about you---that you want some monetary gains from them; that you want to destroy their families . . .?"

Even after just these few rhetorical questions, Patience could see the wattage on the light bulb of understanding grow brighter and brighter in Jessie's eyes. Patience was certain she had called all these issues as ones Jessie and her family had questioned about her.

". . . and then . . ." Patience continued, " . . . when they can't fight the question of your blood anymore, they then question your worthiness; 'is she worthy of being embraced by this family'. I suspect, Jessie that were I not on my A game professionally, there might have been a little less embracing of Patience Bright. If I were the welfare queen with five children and living in public housing, I'm not sure that I would have been welcomed here . . . at least not by everybody".

Jessie sat quietly as she took in all Patience was saying. She had to admit, she thought to herself, that what her sister spoke, albeit unflattering, was the truth. Patience saw the glint of comprehension in the relaxing of Jessie's facial muscles and the unfurrowing of her brows.

"It was the unknowing that actually drove me to put everything into my career and into preparing for my career after the Army. I worked and I worked . . . harder than anybody else I've ever known. I took on every conceivable assignment; volunteered for the tours out in the middle of nowhere. I thought if I focused all my energies on work I wouldn't feel that void. That emptiness . . . that not knowing . . . this big question mark was like a ghost that just kept haunting me. I added school on top of work and finished all three of my degrees in record time, and with a perfect GPA. The more I accomplished . . . the more I tried to put the question of my identity out of my mind, the more it nagged me, and the more profoundly it nagged me. I felt like a person running on a treadmill . . . I just couldn't get away from it, Jessie".

Patience inhaled, then exhaled laboriously. She looked up towards the ceiling, and Jessie knew it was to avert the tears Jessie had already seen teasing at the rim of her eyelids. Jessie reached across the twelve or so inches that separated the two women, and took Patience's hands into her own two hands. Patience swallowed hard, then continued explaining that to which Jessie, up to now, seemed oblivious.

"When I was up against a brick wall, so to speak, there was still that wide gaping hole in my life. Having a baby didn't even fill it up. In fact, that may have made the hole even wider, but certainly deeper. Now I needed to know who I was so I could tell him who he was" Patience explained, then continued.

"I met my father . . . our father; and your mother, my aunt" Patience smiled, then proceeded. ". . .she embraced me warmly and we shared a special moment just about a week before they died. Aunt Angeline . . ."

A sudden hitch of emotions rose up in Jessie's throat at hearing Patience call her mother 'Aunt Angeline'. She patted her chest before getting up from her chair and hugging the woman who was her sister as well as her first cousin. The impromptu hug went on for in excess of a minute, with both women's eyes spilling over warm tears. They sat back down and Patience picked up where she had left off before Jessie's emotional eruption.

" . . . she assured me that I looked just like my mother. That was comforting. Now, I don't know how she dealt with her husband about my existence, and that's not something I necessarily want to know. It just felt good that she opened her heart to me; that she didn't blame me".

"Aunt Mary said Mama knew . . ." Jessie said with downcast eyes.

"Does that make you sad, Jess?" Patience asked.

"I don't know, Patience. I don't know. Remember earlier when Millicent was so casual about Daddy's carousing?" Jessica asked.

"Yeah . . ." Patience said with a half smile/half laugh.

"I wasn't sure how to feel about that. In fact I was feel'in some type 'a way for a minute, but then, I . . ." Patience started.

". . . what do you mean you were feel'in some type 'a way?" Jessie inquired, again, with naivete etched on her face.

". . .well . . . I was just hoping . . . I don't know . . ." Patience shrugged, then frowned slightly.

"C'mon, Patience, talk to me . . ." Jessie prompted.

As Patience looked Jessie in the eye, she remembered how Millicent had deadpanned: *'The fact is, Patience, we were more shocked by who Daniel's mother was than by who your father was"*.

"The words still shock me Jessie. Maybe shock isn't the right word . . ." Patience put the index finger of her right hand up to her lip, then amended her feelings.

". . .disappointment. That's a truer description of what I felt when Millicent said that. I just wasn't prepared to hear that. I suppose children, even grown up ones, always hope for something close to perfection from their parents. . ."

Patience raised her right hand in defense of what she was saying and proceeded with an explanation.

". . . I know that's not realistic for any human being, but we tend to hope for a higher standard of being from the people who create us. After all, if they're good, that means that their products are good, right? I had hoped for something more flattering about the man who fathered me. I had gotten the blunt end of my life story from the mouths of a family who had been hurt and constantly humiliated by my mother. They hated her, so naturally they didn't have anything good to say about her. I am not at all naïve to the less than graceful details of how I was conceived, but I suppose I still hoped for some shred of moral fiber from at least one side of my DNA. I just found it disturbing that his own daughters---the daughters who grew up in the household and who had access to him everyday--- could speak so casually of his unfaithfulness to his wife. I guess I expected my dad's legitimate children to be protective of an image, albeit distorted, of perfection".

Patience shrugged her shoulders despairingly, then added,

" . . .but given that my mother was my father's sister-in-law and that they made at least two children together, I have to step back and take inventory of how unrealistic I've been . . . I mean what's before me is what's before me; it is what it is".

"That's why I said I was sad . . .I'm sad, Patience, because that's what we lived with. No, we didn't have to fend for ourselves and we always knew we had the safety of home and a daddy and a mama to do what mama's and daddy's are supposed to do. No, I won't pretend, not for a second that I can compare our challenges to your challenges growing up. But we all knew. No, we didn't know about you, per se, but we all knew that daddy ran around on mama all our lives. And to make matters worse, we knew that mama knew. It was as if there was this deal between them---'you take care of me and you can have free reign; all the women you want'".

Jessica squinted her eyes and continued sharing her feelings. "I'm saddened by the fact that our father had so little respect for Mama that he slept with her sister; that he had what looks like an on-going sexual relationship with his wife's sister . . . and the fact that Mama raised a child that her husband fathered with her sister, and yet she continued on with this façade of normalcy. That makes me not just sad, but afraid".

". . .afraid ?" Patience asked.

"Yeah. Afraid. Mama was our model; she's the one that taught us how to be wives; all of us . . . all six of us will take the cues that she gave us to know how to engage with our husbands." Jessica said.

". . . and you're afraid that . . .?" Patience started, but before she could finish the question Jessica was already answering it with a sure, but slow nod of her head.

"I'm already seeing it. I'm seeing it and I see the misery it's causing my sisters. On the other hand, though, I have no business being in their business".

Patience looked at Jessie and the two women bonded in some spiritual way.

Jessie added, " . . . plus you know I have to wonder about us . . . about me . . . about all of us. We grew up believing we came from something that was really a fantasy . . . our mother's fantasy. I have to wonder what is real . . . what was real in our lives. I have to wonder who we are. I think my mother tried so hard to forget about how she grew up that she did actually forget; she did more than forget, she created a whole 'nother world. How important was that fantasy for her . . . that . . . that she . . . that she got totally lost in what was real and what wasn't . . . that she was willing to compromise every shred of dignity to keep up a farce of a marriage. Was Mama that desperate for what looked like a family that she would try to make one out of clay? Was she so caught up in this fantasy of hers that she accepted Daddy's blatant disrespect for her as a woman . . . as his wife? You gotta' know that having children with your wife's sister is off-the-chart ugly. . . and that he did it twice and she accepted it twice just places a big question mark on my respect for my mother . . . and no, this isn't about judging Mama . . . it's that I almost feel sorry for her . . ."

Just as Jessie uttered the last words of her statement the phone alarm chirped piercingly, startling both women back to reality.

". . . shoot, what time is it?" Patience asked as he looked around at the partially bluing skies.

"Oh, Lord, we've been up all night!" Jessie confirmed.

"I had my alarm set for 5:45 so I could call and wake my girls up for school".

"Listen, we'd better get a few minutes of shut-eye or we're going to be a wreck today. Funerals around here are a big deal. They can go on for hours" Jessie warned before she traipsed off to a bedroom in the back of the house.

Chapter 27

$\mathbf{D}$aniel remembered rising early on the morning of Aunt Mary's service.   He doesn't remember that he slept a wink the night before, and yet he was not tired at all.   He smiled as he remembered the joy of the night before; how he and four of his sisters had sat up well into the night, laughing and reminiscing, and teaching one another about who they were, and more importantly about who they had become.

"We are grown people now. . ." he thought to himself, before adding, " . . . like the branches of the oak, we come from a common place, but we all have taken on new identities; our own identities. . . forged by the persons we aspire to be".

Daniel held the coffee mug firmly in his hands, watching the steam from the hot brew rise up and waft into his nostrils, comforting him, even from its aroma.   He smiled inwardly as he thought about the inspiration they all gathered from Patience telling her story of perseverance; how she had worked hard and achieved against all conceivable odds, and yet had remained humble.

As Daniel peered boldly into the eastern skies he discovered that he was no longer tormented by exhaustion or depression or anger or any of the emotional burdens that had afflicted him for longer than he cared to remember. His experience of sharing openly and honestly and without fear of judgment in the presence of Dr. Matthews had brought him to a place of peace with what he needed to do next. He understood that the work ahead of him would not be easy, but he now had the resolve to take charge of his life and to make it what *he* wanted it to be. He was ready, he realized, to define his own destiny, as opposed to the destiny defined by his mother's legacy of shame or his father's history of wanting to bring honor to his name. He was ready to be Daniel for Daniel's sake; not the sake of sisters who needed to play mama with his life, or aunties who needed him to remember his place.

Daniel faced the bright seven AM sun with a cup of soothing coffee and the opportunity to reflect on where he would go from here. Sitting on the glider in the brisk, but comfortable early October mist of the low country, Daniel was not afraid to take inventory of his life anymore; was not afraid to own where he had gone wrong or to acknowledge the wrong he had inflicted upon those he should have loved and protected. As if he were the one to be interred in a few hours, Daniel's life flashed before him like an old reel-to-reel movie. Amidst the sweet harmony of the singing blue jays, cardinals, and mourning doves that flitted back and forth from tree to tree, a man comes to terms with himself for himself.

Daniel considered his children, first and foremost . . . his own flesh and blood, and how he had been dismissing of them; how he had believed that sending money was enough to make him a good father, or to make him a father at all. He considered how he had chosen one as meriting his time and attention, solely because his family had believed her mother had come from the 'right' place; a place, ironically, that was starkly opposite from where they, themselves, had come.

The videotape that is his mind rolled back to 1992 when a just barely twenty-one year old got the call from his hometown sweetheart. Daniel remembered that as much as he cared about Carla, he knew from their first reaction years earlier that his choice of a girlfriend, even in high school, had not met either his parents' or his sisters' approval. He remembered the comments as clearly if it was only yesterday.

". . . boy that ain't the kind of girl you want to associate with" his mother had warned.

"What's wrong with her" he had asked innocently.

"That girl live way out there in the country; her family ain't got noth'in son, and they don't want noth'in; they 'bout dumb as tree stumps out there" his mother had responded.

Although this conversation occurred what seems like two lifetimes ago, Daniel could still recall vividly how his eyebrow had furrowed at his mother's response to his naïve question.

"Son, listen to me . . ." his mother had stated with a little more inflection and a lot more octave in her voice, ". . . you need to be wit' somebody who come from someth'in; your daddy been in the Army for twenty years. We got a nice house in a nice subdivision; you and your sisters never want for noth'in in your life . . . mess wit' them little hussies from out there in that country, next thing you know they done put them roots on you . . . believe me, son, she gon' be more of a liability than anything else. Leave her alone".

Daniel remembered hearing the last statement as an order rather than a suggestion.

So, while his heart kept him with Carla in secret, his mind, and his mother's edict, told him that the relationship would only be the kind that would be undertaken in the dark of night. He had met Carla at school, and he had fallen in tenth-grade love with her at first sight. He remembered that she was smart, pretty, and had the most beautiful smile he had ever seen. Her teeth were perfectly white and she had cheekbones that lifted to meet a sparkle in her eyes that he had never seen in another person's eyes since. He remembered that they had spent countless hours on the phone until ungodly hours of the night. When he left for boot camp he asked her to wait for him even though he knew then that he could never have made her his wife.

Daniel shook his head in shame as he recalled how, rather than stepping up and talking with Carla himself, he had relinquished responsibility for his child's life to his parents. The handy excuse he had told himself was that he was away serving his country. To this day, his face still stung with the bite of shame as he recalled running into Carla on one of his visits to Bristol Creek. Her belly was just rounding out in what he calculated would have been about her fifth month. He saw the hurt and disappointment in her eyes as he flaunted his new wife in a visit to Bristol Creek. He remembered that he had turned his head to avoid saying hello to the young woman who was carrying his child. Ironically, Daniel recalled, he had made the trip all the way from Louisiana to celebrate his sister, Nina's baby, while he denied or ignored his own.

When Daniel told his parents about Carla's pregnancy, Tan and Angeline had assured their adult baby (son) that they would take care of this 'little matter'. When their efforts to get Carla to abort the fetus fell on deaf ears, it had been Tan and

Angeline Francis who had diligently sent a check to Carla each month. Neither they nor Daniel had ever, in twenty-one years, expressed an inkling of an interest in seeing or connecting with Blade. Daniel admitted to himself, shamefully, that he had often wondered about his first born---how he was doing; what he was doing; who he looked like; did he have any of the Francis idiosyncrasies---but that he had never been man enough to stand up to his own family. . . not even to his parents . . . especially not to his parents. He had always allowed his family to make his decisions---if they said it was not okay, then he accepted that as the gospel. As he sat on the front porch on this morning, Daniel faced the blistering morning sun and himself. He acknowledged, for the first time, that he, and he alone, was to blame for his irresponsibility towards Blade.

Daniel recalled that his parents' response to him having gotten involved with a girl of Carla Mabry's caliber was that they needed to intervene in his life in order to help him set his life straight. That he had defied her directive about associating with Carla, and that she had gotten pregnant was evidence, his mother reasoned, of precisely what she had warned: that Carla would be a liability for him. Because she deemed herself to have been right, she was even more apt, now, to remind him that he needed her to direct his life if he was to amount to anything.   In no time at all, it seemed, Angeline had maneuvered an introduction and within a few months of Carla's announcement of her pregnancy, Daniel was standing at the altar with Victoria Elsey. It was the perfect picture, he remembered---the pretty petite bride and her handsome groom decked out in his Army dress greens.

". . . now, they will make pretty children and their children will be respectable, too. . ." he could imagine his parents saying. Even on this day, Daniel can remember how he stood at the altar on that day as if he had merely been plopped into a role. . .as if he was given an assignment, and like a good soldier, was bound and determined to do as he was instructed with no questions asked. This life, he remembered, was to be his saving grace. . . a girl from the right side of the tracks; a girl whose father was a military man; a girl who would help him get his life on track; someone to save him from his stupid self. The problem was, Daniel reminded himself, that in the eyes of the Elsey family he was nothing; he was the same to them as Carla was to the Francis family. He recalled always jumping through proverbial hoops to be accepted . . . to be seen as worthy, and yet he knew he could never be an Elsey. In fact he wasn't even sure that he wanted to be an Elsey.

Daniel recalled that his almost four-year marriage to Vickie Elsey felt to him like a thousand years at the bottom rung of Dante's inferno. Throughout their marriage he had always been Vickie's project; something for her to smooth out, refine, make presentable. Vickie had no problem reminding him of what he needed to do to be better----better at earning rank; better at managing his troops; better at dressing; better at hobnobbing with the 'right' people; better at being a husband; better at being a lover; better at being a father to Sheila . . . better at being like her own father. By the time their divorce was final, Daniel wasn't sure who he was or who he was supposed to be. He only knew that whoever or whatever he was, was simply inadequate. He felt worthless, yet wrung out and exhausted.

As the tape fast forwarded to 1996 Daniel saw a replay of just four years prior. At the age of twenty-five he had a pregnant wife and a pregnant girlfriend. One he loved with every fiber of his being and the other he hated just as intensely. In stark resistance to his parents' edict, he married Aisha although, like Carla, she was from the wrong part of town. Daniel recalled, though, that this time he was not going to allow his parents to choose for him; he was going to marry Aisha, if anything, precisely because his family despised her. He was determined to prove them wrong; he could make something of Aisha; he was dead set on making his new wife a lady; to show her the finer things in life; to help her appreciate something other than blindingly long false eye lashes, leopard print stilettos and gold teeth. He had come to enjoy Aisha's moxie. She dared to challenge his mother and his sisters when he hadn't the backbone to do so. It wasn't long into the marriage before he realized that he had put Aisha on the front lines of his battle for himself. His wife was in a constant wrestling match with his family. She butted head with his parents, his sisters, and his values, and by the time Sienna was born less than two years later, the demise of the marriage was looming. The haunting reality for Daniel was that there were two children who suffered the fall out: Parker and Sienna. While Sienna had always been warm and welcoming to her daddy's visit, Parker had come to reject him coldly. As Parker came into adolescence especially, it seems the two of them had become enemies. Daniel wasn't sure when or how it started, since the child had been so young during what turned out to be a pretty bitter divorce, but along the way he knew his son hated him. In reaction to everything Daniel stood for, Parker had done just the opposite. Parker shunned his visits; Parker was truant in school; and he had even had a few brushes with the law and had spent time in the juvenile justice system. Daniel feared for what would happen to his son; he feared his son becoming yet another statistic---dead or incarcerated. He prayed hard and often that God would show him how to reach his child; how to make amends and connect before it was too late.

By the time he was nearing his fourth decade Daniel realized that he had not done much better. On the northern side of his thirties, and with a fifth child on the way, Daniel came to realize sitting on the front porch swing, that he had still been hiding behind anybody who would assume responsibility for his life. While he wouldn't have normally considered his partner relationships and his children as victims, his recent acceptance of the onus for his deeds and misdeeds served the secondary purpose of having clarified for him that most, if not all, of the people in the relationships he pursued were victims, indeed. They existed in his life for the sole purpose of providing him a shield behind which to hide from growing up. He had not brought Holly or Frisco around his family for fear they would, in usual fashion, be critical of his choices.

Daniel considered that in all of this he held no ill feelings towards his family. A decade ago he would have pointed the finger at them. . .at all of them, for the choices he had made. Today, however, on this Thursday morning, he, the grown-up (or growing up) Daniel didn't. On this morning, he held Daniel responsible for Daniel's life, which he knew is precisely what assured him that he had the power to turn it around.

Chapter 28

"**P**hew!   What! A! Sendoff!" Jackie shouted with wild exuberance.

"You got that right!" Patience seconded enthusiastically, then added, ". . . my God, I don't know that I've ever been to a funeral like that! . . . it was awesome".

"I only wish I could go out with a bang like that" Millicent lamented.

"You talk about a full house! Standing room only doesn't begin to describe that place. It was packed! And people were outside the church who never even got inside" Jessie noted.

". . . and if anybody deserved it, its Aunt Mary" Daniel said. Five of Tan Francis' children who had just attended their aunt's funeral returned to the Francis homestead to disrobe and decompress after a long and emotionally charged service. Even amidst the rave reviews of their aunt's funeral, Daniel's sisters couldn't help but notice that their brother seemed preoccupied. While Millicent, Jessie, and Jackie assumed their brother's mood to be about grief----grief over Aunt Mary's passing, as well as the continued grief they, too, were feeling about their parents' shocking death just a little over a year ago. Patience wasn't sure what was so distracting to Daniel. It could very well have been grief, but she suspected that at least one other issue may have factored into the aura of uneasiness that was so evident in Daniel's countenance.

" . . . and they don't call it a funeral, I noticed. Everybody that spoke, and even the program has 'home-going services' written on it" Patience observed.

With at least four pairs of pumps strewn across the living room floor and eight stocking-clad legs draped across the arms of the sofa, arm chairs and recliners, the women merely nodded their understanding of the notion of a home-going service as opposed to a funeral. Jessie offered her perspective on the change of name for a person's final service.

"I think the word funeral carries such a negative connotation; like this was the end, when, if you're a Christian, you really believe . . . you actually *know* that this isn't the end at all; you know you're really going home to be with the Lord . . . and God knows everybody--- at least everybody in these parts--- knows that Aunt Mary has a spot in heaven".

"Yes Lord!" Millicent echoed.

"Aunt Mary was an awesome woman" Jessica stated. "She was always the quiet one of Mama's sisters. She didn't make a lot of noise like Aunt Sarah and them".

"Yeah . . ." Daniel drawled in a deep gravely voice. He added, ". . . but more than that, she was always doing something to help somebody, ya' know . . . and all along, she was always quiet about what she did for you. If you had a problem, Aunt Mary was going to help you out of it . . . but she was going to read you first" Daniel laughed.

". . . sound like you know from first hand experience, Junie" Jackie hinted.

"Yeah! Yeah I know. Sssshhh, I can't count the times Aunt Mary done save my teenage behind from hot water. But she wasn't gonna' do anything illegal, though. . . and if you were wrong, you couldn't get her to participate in it; she wasn't going to do anything that was gonna hurt anybody. She was just a good person", Daniel concluded.

"Well, when you think about all the testimonials today, it was obvious she had a good heart, and her goodness didn't stop with her family. People loved her, that's for sure", Jessica declared.

"Oh, yeah . . ." Millicent confirmed, ". . .today is Thursday! People don't take off from work and come to a funeral in the middle of the week like this. That alone was evidence of what Aunt Mary meant to the people of this community".

"You're right . . ." Jessie said, nodding her head slowly and looking contemplative.

". . .and who was that fellow in the military uniform?" Jackie asked with a far away look on her face.

Jessie shrugged casually, but offered a suggestion.

"The name tag said Milledge. Must be one of Aunt Ruby or Aunt Sarah's grandsons. Fine young man. Intelligent. Spoke well and obviously thought the world of Aunt Mary".

Her sister's speculation didn't add up for Jackie. She was trying with all her might to figure out the identity of the Army officer who's thunderous voice and eloquent diction captured the attention and moved the heart of every person in the church.

". . .but none of them last name is Milledge . . . I mean none of their kids' last name was Milledge", Jackie noted with furrowed brows.

". . . truth be told I can't imagine any of them young'uns doing nothing productive like going in the Army . . . but who ever he belong to, they should be proud . . . and from his looks, he's family, alright" Millicent offered cynically.

"Fella is an officer . . . got a firm grip. Solid young man" Daniel said almost to himself, and while looking at no one in particular.

". . .an officer?" Jackie asked, then shook her head skeptically.

"Nah . . .I'm trying to remember, but heck there's so many of them kids . . . Aunt Ruby and Aunt Sarah together must have had about seven or eight kids . . . none of the girls went to college, and all of the boys went to prison. Maybe that's one of Uncle Jessie's grandkids" Jackie surmised.

Patience noticed that everybody nodded their head, deciding that Lt. Milledge had to be one of Uncle Jessie's grandsons . . . everybody except Daniel.

Daniel's distraction was becoming more and more pronounced, with the sisters starting to make eye conversations with one another as an indication of their concern for their brother.

Daniel's mind drifted to the recession and the receiving line at the home-going service. He had seen the name Lt. Frank Milledge, USA on the program as one of the persons offering reflections. He also remembered how nimble and crisp the young man articulated his words; how impassioned he seemed to have been about Aunt Mary; and that he was wearing the uniform of a United States Army officer. Daniel considered further that the young man seemed to have known the deceased very well. In fact he called her his honorary grandmother.

Daniel had rarely if ever put much stock in what he called his sister's crazy female ideas about feelings. They were always talking about feeling connections with people, and he had always found their talk laughable. In fact he recalled just the day before how Jackie and Jessie had called him out about having not felt a connection with Patience when they met in 1992.   Today, however, at the funeral, he believed he experienced precisely what he had thumped his nose at; he believed he felt something. . . Daniel couldn't name what he had experienced, but he knew he felt something akin to electricity flow through his entire body when Frank Milledge shook his hand as he passed through the receiving line. In fact, he was taken aback when the young man not only shook his hand, but pulled him into a strong, but warm embrace. The hug, he remembered, was cordial, but genuine; it was warm and loving, but exuded strength. There was something about the hug, Daniel remembered, that had moved him to tears. He couldn't identify it precisely, but was sure there was something in his engagement with Lt. Frank Milledge that drew intense emotions out of him.

". . . earth to Daniel . . . earth to Daniel Francis . . ."

Daniel shook himself out of the trance that had consumed him as his sisters eyed him suspiciously. They had taken a break from debating the possible parentage of the mystery family member to check on him.

"Are you okay, June?" Jessie asked with genuine concern.

"Yeah" Daniel lied.

Satisfied with their brother's fabricated declaration that he was feeling fine, Daniel's sisters resumed their deliberations regarding Lt. Milledge's genealogy. Daniel noticed that at least three of his four sisters seemed to have become suddenly obsessed with how the young Army officer figured into their family; whose son he could be; and how he had become so enamored with Aunt Mary. Daniel noticed also that Patience wasn't participating in the discussion, but rather that she had trained her hazel eyes on him with a hard and burdened look.

"I'm a member of this family now, right?" Patience asked no one in particular.

"Really, Patience? . . ." Jessie challenged, ". . . do you really need to confirm your place in this family?"

Before the ensuing din of everybody's contributions to a question meant to be entirely rhetorical, Patience waved her right hand in surrender.

"Okay, okay, guys. No offense intended, but y'all are wondering so hard about Frank. . ."

She looked at Daniel again, this time with eyes even more laden with anxiety than just a few seconds earlier.

"Daniel . . ." Patience started tentatively, then looked around at Millicent, Jackie, and Jessie. ". . . did y'all hear what Frank said in his eulogy of Aunt Mary?".

Although this question begged an actual reply, no one in the room ventured a response. Rather, they merely looked around at one another, befuddled, before Jackie remembered Frank Milledge's reference to the deceased as his honorary grandmother. Patience nodded affirmatively as did Daniel, Millicent, and then, Jessie. Then, as if on a scavenger hunt, everybody else in the room, except Daniel, started wrestling with their memories for snippets of the young soldier's passionate tribute to the deceased.

". . . he said something about Aunt Mary giving him a name" Millicent said. The excitement started building in the room as each person threw in bits and pieces of Lt. Milledge's speech amidst yelling and wild guessing. They even started tossing their hands up in the air as if they were second graders who had come up with the correct answers and couldn't wait to share it with the entire classroom.

". . . yeah, and I remember he said something about when he and his mama didn't have nobody . . ." Jessie contributed.

". . . see . . ." Jackie confirmed, ". . . I can't imagine any of Uncle Jessie's grandchildren ever feeling like they didn't have anybody; they would have always had Uncle Jessie and Aunt Frances. . . so, that just don't sound right".

Still on a hunt in her mind, Jackie scratched her head and contorted her face.

Patience nodded her head to inform Jackie that she was on the right path, or rather that it was right of her to abandon the path she had been on before; that Frank was *not* one of Uncle Jessie's grandsons. She looked at Daniel again and prompted him.

". . . Aunt Mary gave him a name . . ."

"Oh! Oh! I know . . ." Jessie offered jumping to her feet and pacing the room in deep thought, " . . . he didn't have a name. . . that's it. . . *he didn't have a name*! That was old fashion speak for when a child was born out of wedlock!"

"Yeah! That's right! So we know Frank was born to a woman who was not married . . . and . . . and . . ." Jackie started.

". . .and they had nobody!" Jessie added, tapping the side of her temples as she paced the room, " . . . so that would mean Aunt Mary took them in . . ."

". . . and that's what the honorary grandmother is about!" Jackie shot.

Jackie, Jessie, and Millicent were deep in thought as if they were playing a game of charades. They tapped their temples, contorted their faces, and paced up and down the room, trying out mumbled guesses on themselves before shouting them to the group as a whole.

Patience looked piercingly at Daniel and said very slowly, "she gave him a name when he didn't have one . . ."

". . .so, since she didn't have any children of her own and had never married, maybe . . ." Jessie ventured, but abandoned the idea before completing her thought.

Daniel's eyes perked up, and for the first time in this guessing game he spoke up slowly and in an eerily low voice.

". . .so . . ." he spoke tentatively, at first, ". . . she may have given the child the name Milledge . . . the child didn't have to be a Milledge by birth; Aunt Mary may have given the child that name".

Daniel stood up, and walked towards the door, then made a sharp circle back and stood in front of Patience. His eyes pierced into hers like daggers. He squatted down in front of his youngest sister and placed each one of his hands on Patience's shoulders. Patience's eyes met her brother's with as much, if not more, intensity than what he exuded. They were locked brown eye-to-brown eye . . .soldier-to-soldier, with no one relenting. It felt to Patience like a stand-off, but one that she needed and one that she knew Daniel also needed. . . this would be a standoff with positive outcomes. This was the last of the secrets Patience had to share. It was not her intent to have revealed her nephew's identity in this forum or in this manner, but the one thing this entire process had taught her was that she simply could not rehearse how to give people life changing information. When Daniel spoke in a low and deliberate drone, Patience knew she had finally hit pay dirt.

With both his hands firmly planted on Patience's shoulders and with their eyes locked into one another Daniel jumped back into the fray, but with an unabashed demand from his youngest sister. "You got to know Aunt Mary very well, Pat. She told you a lot of family secrets . . . a hell of a lot of family secrets. She would have told you about Frank".

Daniel's statement sounded more like an accusation than a guess at who Frank's parents might be.

"She did" Patience confirmed, tersely, holding Daniel's eyes.

"What do you know about that boy?" Daniel asked pointedly.

"What I know is that you need to take care of your business" Patience answered just as pointedly, but, in a soft, supportive tone.

Jessie, Jackie, and Millicent looked on in suspense as Daniel's hands left the crown of Patience's shoulders and his arms wrapped around her neck. Given the tone the two had assumed in their brief, but intense, exchange, Jessie, Jackie, and Millicent couldn't be certain whether or not Daniel's grasp of Patience would have resulted in a caress or a charge. All three of the women looked on in awe as the two hugged one another with all their might. Confusion was evident in every crevice of the three women's faces, showing in their questioning eyes, in their furrowed brows, in their slackened jaws, and in their speechlessness.

Without a word to anyone except a 'thank you' to Patience, Daniel grabbed the keys to his rental car and made a mad dash for the front door.

Chapter 29

Daniel drove tentatively down the long rutted dirt path. As he looked around at the tangled Jasmine racing to the top of the tall pine trees, he smiled remembering the flowers' sweet perfume. He remembered thinking it strange that the state's flower bloomed twice a year out on the country, when where he lived in the suburbs, they only saw the yellow flowers in early spring. He recalled also that while in the burbs they saw, but could barely smell the flower, while in the country the scent of the jasmine was at least a hundred times more aromatic, especially at dusk. He could recall how he had sat on the Mabry's old front porch and inhaled the Jasmine's perfume on the night air. That soft scent, along with the piercing night sounds of the crickets and the cicadas, had endeared him to this part of Bristol Creek. He remembered also that he had been fascinated with the fireflies that he saw out there that he had never seen where he lived just twenty minutes away. Daniel came close to laughter as he remembered his father's explanation for the wonders he saw in the rural parts of the county that he had never experienced in the suburbs. As if the works of nature warranted a warning rather than simple appreciation, his father had cautioned him that " . . . strange things happen out there in them woods".

He drove along slowly, with his right foot hovering just over the car's brake pedal. All four windows of the rented Tahoe were open, as Daniel took in the crisp smell of green pine needles, mixed in with the aroma of oak and maple leaves burning somewhere in the distance. In that instant he came to realize that not a lot had changed . . . at least not this far out in the country. Homes were still separated by acres and acres of fields with crops waiting to be harvested; and everybody still waved at every passing car, as if every vehicle were that of their next door neighbor. The birds still sung freely and loudly, and people enjoyed a simple and carefree lifestyle, unburdened by security guards, gated communities, homeowner association rules, or pretentiousness.

He easily spotted the old homestead---a white-washed cinderblock house with faded blue make-shift shutters. The front porch always had the look of not being a part of the house. Somehow it looked to Daniel like the roof of the front porch was slanted downward as if it would separate from the house with a good puff of wind. Strange, Daniel thought, how the cornfields seemed to surround the house in every direction. The front yard consisted of cornfields, as did every piece of land on either side of the house.

As Daniel pulled up in front of the house, an old man with scraggly tufts of snow white hair hobbled out of the front door and across the rickety porch. The old fellow held on to a two-x- four that connected the porch floor to its sagging roof. He clumsily descended the un-cemented stack of cinder blocks that served as risers, and made his way right up to the car door. Although the old man was already standing at the driver side door of the SUV by the time he could get the vehicle in park, Daniel, parked and exited the vehicle, anyway. He extended his hand and the old fellow accepted the handshake with an equally firm grip.

"How you do'in sir?"

"Just fine young man, how 'bout you?"

"Doing well sir. I'm . . ."

Daniel started at an introduction, but before he could identify himself the old man interrupted.

"I know who you is, son . . . and I want'cha' to know I'm 'a keep yo family in prayer . . . about yo aunt . . . Miss Mary . . . nice lady. God rest her soul . . . we sho gon miss her round here. Real nice Christian lady . . .yeah".

Daniel noticed that despite John Mabry's, age, and the pipe perched soundly between his tightly clenched teeth, the old man spoke clearly. Daniel inhaled the scent of Old Man John Mabry's Applewood tobacco, and for a moment he was gripped by nostalgia. He couldn't help but remember the evenings he and the old man sat out on the front porch shucking corn while the old man inundated him with farming stories. Daniel remembered that Carla's father's constant presence was a part of the courting ritual in the rural areas. After he had officially asked to keep company with Old Man Mabry's daughter, maintaining a watchful eye on the two youngsters was a staple until the father felt he could trust 'that boy from town' with his only daughter. As he got a whiff of the tobacco smoke wafting through the air, Daniel remembered that there was something peaceful in the scent of the tobacco--- a calm; a quiet; a solitude that he, even as a teenager, had come to appreciate.

Embarrassment and shame colored Daniel's head and neck a bright red. He really hadn't thought this through at all, he realized. If he had, he probably would have lost his courage. He knew better than anybody else, that he had no business here. He had left this man's young daughter pregnant and never looked back. As he stood here, self contempt kept him from looking into Mr. Mabry's age faded eyes.

Daniel looked down, shuffling his feet in the dirt yard.

"Mr. Mabry, I'm try'in to find Carla. Can you help me get in touch with her?" Daniel asked.

Old man Mabry perched his right hand hard onto the cane that supported his ambulation. He used his left hand to remove the pipe from his mouth.

"Well, son, I don't know if da' gal got too much she want'a say to you, but dat' aint none a' my business. I reckon I can tell you how to get to her place. Go on round da' house, ya' so; pass da' last cornfield, shru da' clear'in . . ." he twisted his body around and pointed in a north westerly direction over the roof of his own house, " . . . and you'll see her place ova' dey".

"Thank you sir. Thank you very much, sir" Daniel said, genuinely grateful and yet still feeling like a fool for coming here. As Daniel got back into the shiny black Tahoe, and maneuvered slowly in the direction of Carla Mabry's house, it dawned on him that he didn't have a clue what he was going to say to Carla.

He had gotten past the first hurdle, but suddenly realized that he was only at the foot of this mountain. The crags he had before him were likely going to be a lot sharper and a lot more difficult to climb than his encounter with his son's grandfather. He hit the brakes as it occurred to him that he had no idea what he was walking into. He had absolutely no idea what Carla's life was like---was she married? . . . and if so, how would her husband feel about him just popping up after twenty one years? . . . was she angry? . . . had she told their son about him?. All these fears and apprehension ate away at his courage as he sat there in a brand spanking new vehicle idling at the intersection of two single lane dirt roads lined by miles and miles of swaying stalks of fall corn.

Daniel eventually put the car in 'D' again and acknowledged to himself that he probably only drove on because he knew beyond any doubt that the man who pulled him into a hug was his son; his flesh and blood. He knew it in his soul. . . he knew it when Frank pulled him into an embrace at the church; he knew it even as his sisters wracked their brains trying to assign his son a paternity. It was this knowledge, albeit unproven, that fueled his continued movement in the direction of the unknown.   He also knew that his son's name was Milledge, and that Aunt Mary had stepped up as the honorable person when neither he nor his parents ever did the right thing. He wasn't sure if Carla would even have a conversation with him, but at this point, there was no turning back. As he drove seven miles per hour down the winding lane, Daniel realized that he needed to remove his parents from the equation.

"Yes, they ignored my child . . . but I ignored my child" he reminded himself.

Without notice the clearing opened, and there before him was a beautiful estate looking home sitting alone in a quiet glade. Daniel noticed the manicured lawn, with bushy tailed squirrels spiraling their way up and down young oaks. He drove onto the black-top driveway and followed its off-white cement trimmed edging around past the three car garage to the front stoop. Daniel was stunned. While he wasn't sure what he expected, this wasn't it. This was not the caliber of structure he would have ever expected this far out in the country. On the other hand, though, he realized that it was probably only on this kind of open space, with mature trees and everything natural, that a house of this caliber would have been accorded any justice. He had never, ever discussed Carla with any member of his family, so he had no idea how her life had turned out; whether she had a career or what. He had only remembered his mother's words that she would be a liability. As he looked at this home on this expansive acreage, he shook his head. He knew that Carla had done well. In fact it seems she had done very well, indeed. For sure, she had done far better than he had.

By the time he reached the front door, Daniel's legs had turned to Jell-o. Fear gripped every part of his body---his throat felt like hot ashes; his stomach muscles clenched; his mouth was dry as the Gobi desert; and his heart raced with fear. Even his eyes felt hot and dry, as he hobbled up the four brick steps to the Tuscan style arched doorway.

Daniel wasn't sure what to expect so he braced himself for the worst. Even as he talked himself up to the doorway he also reminded himself that what he had done to Carla and Blade was nothing short of cowardly. He had left her pregnant, and although he had been in town at least a hundred times in the last two decades he had never once so much as picked up the phone to see how his child was doing. The fact is, he didn't even know his child's name. He had caught wind of the name Blade, and because he had refused to ever discuss the child with anyone, especially his busybody cousins, all he knew was Blade. Based on what he had read in his aunt's funeral program, Blade's name wasn't Blade; his name was Frank. He wasn't even sure when his son's birthday was. As he told himself these things, common sense told him to run . . . to get away from Carla's house. . . but somehow and for reasons unbeknownst even to himself, his legs kept climbing the steps and his index finger even dared to push the doorbell.

Chapter 30

" . . .so she took you in . . .?" Daniel asked in awe.

Carla nodded her head affirmatively.

"If it wasn't for her, our lives would have been very different" Carla said, looking around the spacious great room with its twenty-seven foot ceiling and exposed beams.

Daniel looked down as quiet pervaded the room for what seemed like an eternity before he inhaled and spoke again. Even as he entertained the question in his mind, he thought how ridiculous it sounded. How is it that a man doesn't even know his adult son's own name? "How can that be?" he asked himself, but what he asked Carla was different. Sitting in the wing-back chair he fidgeted as he cringed at the thought of having to ask about Blade's name.

"Blade . . .? . . . Frank. . .? I'm confused. . ." he fumbled.

"I wanted to name him Blade. . ." Carla shrugged and smiled. "I suppose when you're nineteen years old you think of these silly or what you think are hip sounding names for your children. By the time he was born though, Aunt Mary had helped me see the error of that line of thinking. She thought it was important that a boy . . . a man's first son. . . have his name. She didn't have the right to give Blade the Francis name as a sir name, so Francis is his given name. Of course, that quickly became Frank. His full name is Francis Mabry Milledge. . . so we settled on Blade as a nickname".

Carla smiled proudly as she peered at the photograph of her son at his commissioning ceremony. She continued briefing Blade's father on the relationship she and the child had with Daniel's Aunt Mary.

"She had never had any children of her own, had never contributed to the family line, she would always say, so the gift I could give to her was to allow my son to be her grandson. By allowing Blade to carry her name I would honor her forever . . . plus he has Milledge blood coursing through his veins, Daniel" Carla explained.

As Daniel sat before the mother of his first born he beamed with pride and at the same time he was tormented by his own shame. He was honored to be sitting in her presence; grateful that she had done such a phenomenal job in raising their child. He was thankful that Carla hadn't slammed the door in his face, or better yet, that she didn't spit in his face for having the nerve to darken her door step with his presence. When he thought about how disgracefully he had treated Carla, and now how gracious she was behaving towards him, he could only feel small in her presence.

"Carla, I'm not a religious man . . . not by any stretch of the imagination. I only know that there is a God and that He makes miraculous things happen. Even when I was a selfish fool, God put Aunt Mary in your path. No, it wasn't Aunt Mary's job to take care of you or Blade. That was my job, and I turned my back on you. I ask that you please find it in your heart to forgive me . . . not today . . . and maybe not tomorrow, but at some point in your life, please forgive me . . . and please pray for me. I'm on a journey . . . a growth journey. I hope its not too late for me . . ."

Daniel's words drifted off.

"As long as there is life in your body, there is always hope, Daniel" Carla said with definition.

Daniel's Adam's apple bobbed several times. Carla knew he was struggling to manage his emotions, so she directed the conversation to a slightly different path.

"Blade told me he saw you today".

Both Daniel's mouth and his eyes flew open in amazement.

"Did he know who I was?" he asked.

"Yeah" Carla answered casually.

After a while, Daniel rose from his seat and walked over to the thick wood mantel attached to the stone-front floor-to-ceiling fireplace. There he was introduced to his son through photographs taken at various stages of Blade's life. He realized in that moment that he had missed so much . . . that he had missed so much because of his own immaturity . . . his own irresponsibility. . . his own unwillingness to embrace manhood. Daniel pinched the bridge of his nose but couldn't stop the large drops of tears from crossing over his eye lids. He smiled awkwardly while shaking his head from side to side.

"I'd like to meet him. Do you mind?" Daniel asked with every single one of his words laced with humility.

"Mind?! Are you kidding me! Of course I don't mind. He's your son, Daniel. Regardless of what happened or didn't happen with us, Blade is your boy; you're his father; nothing is going to change that. As a matter of fact he wants to meet you, too" Carla admitted.

"Does he, really?" Daniel asked incredulously.

"Of course he does, Daniel, why wouldn't he?" Carla asked with even more amazement in her voice than what was noted in Daniel's tone.

"Well . . ." Daniel started before Carla cut him off.

"Daniel, we can't rewrite the past. What's done is done. It is what it is. We only have control of the future, and your son wants to be in your future. It is entirely up to you whether or not you want him in your life".

"Carla, that's why I'm here" Daniel said humbly.

"I believe that, and I believe you. I imagine it took a lot for you to ascend those steps today" Carla said with a hint of a smile. Daniel nodded.

"I applaud you for that kind of courage" Carla stated, then proceeded to speak to her son's father about his child.

"Will Blade have questions of you? I suspect he will; but I believe also that you're up to that challenge. If you are courageous enough to come here today, I have no doubt you have what it takes to deal with your son's questions. Is he out to beat you up for not being present in his life?" Carla asked, before answering her own question.

"No. Blade is not that kind of person. Blade is a warm and nurturing person; he is a forgiving person. Your son is spiritual and he understands that everything in life is about growth; that all our experiences help to mold us and move us closer to God's calling for us. He didn't have it bad, Daniel . . .not in terms of growing up in poverty or anything like that. Aunt Mary saw to that, and your parents saw to it that Blade had stuff . . . money. I did very well in my career . . . thanks in large part to Aunt Mary. The only thing that Blade ever wanted was to belong . . . to be embraced . . . to know that from which he sprang . . . and you know what? . . . Aunt Mary and my daddy showered that child with love . . . not stuff, mind you, but love, Daniel. Francis Milledge is not spoiled, but he knows, beyond any doubt, that he was and still is loved".

". . .You call her Aunt Mary. . ." Daniel asked and stated at the same time.

"I should call her 'mama'. . . because that's what she came to mean to me", Carla stated, before she explained further.

". . . you know Daddy never married after Mama died, so I grew up without the benefit of a woman's presence since I was nine. When Aunt Mary learned I was pregnant with her nephew's child, she came out here . . . to the country . . . to my daddy's old broken down shack. She didn't judge; she didn't come out to cast aspersions against dumb country people; and she didn't come out to look down her nose at how we lived. She came out and offered anything along the lines of support. The only thing she asked of me was to not drop out of the tech program I was enrolled in . . . and you know what, Daniel . . . she kept coming and kept coming and kept coming, until she was assured that I was assured that she was sincere. When Blade was born it was me, Aunt Mary, and the nurse in that delivery room".

Daniel was moved by what he was hearing about his aunt. While he had always respected his aunt as a genuinely good person, he really hadn't known the true depths of her goodness. He thought about the good she had done for his family- -how she quietly embraced Patience and supported her through what had to be some of the most difficult challenges of her life; he thought, now, about how she had gone out of her way to take in her nephew's pregnant girlfriend and his child. . . the child the nephew, himself, hadn't bothered to acknowledge. While shame burned through his soul, at the very same time, love warmed his heart. He was warmed and encouraged all at once. He sat in quiet contemplation for a few minutes, absorbing all that Carla had said. He silently thanked God for giving Aunt Mary to Carla and to Blade. He also thanked God for giving him the courage to make a move in the direction of being a man, and he prayed for continued strength. "What do you suggest I do? How should I do this, I mean? I don't know what to do; what to say . . . What have you told him about me?" Before long Daniel realized he had spun off a slew of questions, most of which had little, if any relevance. He realized that he was scared to death about coming face to face with his son. The real paradox was that he feared what he hadn't done as a father and as a man, while simultaneously believing his son, from what he could tell of his behaviors at the service, to be an intelligent and mature gentleman--- everything that he wasn't twenty years ago; and everything that he wasn't even today.

"Whoa . . . slow down . . ." Carla cautioned, ". . .he's just as nervous about meeting you as you are about meeting him. He's nervous about whether he's good enough to be your son; about whether you will accept him as a member of your family . . ."

Carla started, but was interrupted by Daniel.

". . .whether *he's* good enough?!" I am the one who need to make amends here. He pulled his end of the bargain . . . no, he pulled far more than his end of the bargain. I was the one that was not a father and not a man; I am the one that never modeled for him what a man is supposed to be and do, and yet, I saw him stand before a packed congregation today and pay homage to *my* aunt; he did a better job of that than I could have done. It was him donning a uniform that tells me he is making a meaningful career for himself; a career that he had to work hard to achieve, no doubt".

Daniel shook his head as if to wake himself out of a daze.

"No, Carla, this isn't about Blade measuring up; this is about whether or not I will ever be worthy of calling myself his father".

"Daniel, I'm going to keep my nose out of this. This business is between a man and his son. Both of y'all are men, so y'all will do what you need to do.   Blade is at Aunt Mary's. He has to report back to Fort Carson in a few days".

Chapter 31

Before his sisters could figure out Daniel's rapid and unceremonious departure, the six familiar bars of Amazing Grace chimed from the direction of the front door. And despite at least three of Daniel's sisters having heard that doorbell for most of their lives, the sound caused all of the women to startle. At first they all looked at one another as if the bars of the hymn were a condemnation of their very lives. They all looked stunned and at the same time uncomprehending. It was only when the door bell chimed the second time that Jessica rose to answer it.

As she swung the heavy door open, she was surprised to see Lt. Frank Milledge standing on the other side. Less the uniform, the officer still maintained a certain level of decorum. He stood tall and erect and spoke with a certain level of confidence that should not be confused with conceit.

As soon as Blade laid eyes on his aunt, he reached out his right hand in introduction.

"Hello, I'm Frank Milledge" he said in a deep and commanding voice. Jessie shook the young man's hand and invited him in. She looked at him closely and saw the same familiar trait she had tried to identify when she had seen him at the home-going service earlier. Although she couldn't readily articulate what it was, she was certain there was something recognizable about this man. She searched his blunted nose, the smile, even the rounded, slightly puffy light brown eyes, trying to identify that elusive characteristic, but it wouldn't reveal itself.

"Come on in Frank. You're family" Jessie assured.

Before Frank could get his second foot across the door jamb Jackie, Millicent, and Patience had all gone charging to the front door. At the same time, Patience and Jessie both noticed that Daniel's rental had just pulled into the front yard.

"Oh, good, June is back" Jessie declared.

". . . talk about perfect timing . . ." Blade said, " . . . that's just the person I want to see".

Daniel barged through the front door without a clue about Blade's presence. As his father stumbled across the door sill, Blade turned around to meet him eye to eye for the second time that day and for only the second time in his lifetime. The two men stopped, frozen in both place and time. Everything in the room stopped. There was no movement; no sound; no nothing. As recognition tore into her brain like a bolt of lightning, both of Jessica's hands flew to her mouth and a flood of tears washed over her as if a dam had broken behind her eyeballs. Jessie had left home before Daniel came into his prime, but she saw remnants of her teenage brother all over Frank. She knew about Blade, but had never seen him, and had no inkling that the child's real name was Frank.   As Millicent and Jackie, too, realized who Frank Milledge was, Patience saw their trembling hands and their trembling lips. It wouldn't be long before their faces, too, were awash in warm salty tears and viscous mucus.

Even with all that was going on around them, neither Blade nor his father saw or heard any of it; they were each mesmerized by the sheer presence of the other. With not a single word spoken, father and son spoke their own supernatural language; they communicated their knowledge of one another and their love for one another; they spoke silently of a longing to make the metaphysical physical; to make the spiritual concrete. Their eyes danced a dance of comfort and familiarity; of understanding and forgiveness; of the peace and tranquility of belonging . . . of being of one another. Although neither had seen one another before this day, they already knew one another. Theirs was a knowledge that was profound, yet subtle; a wisdom that was tacit; intangible. . . so intrinsic that it needed no words. . . no explanation . . . no justification. A father and his son . . . they knew each other's spirit and could see down to one another's soul.

They both stood frozen for what seemed like an eternity, and then, without words their feet began to move. Like all four of their legs were in some metaphysical sync with each other, the two men simply moved . . . or a better description of what happened is that the two *were* moved. . . carried by some supernatural force towards one another; drawn uncontrollably towards each other like magnet to steel. Like the electricity that coursed through his body earlier in the day, the mere touch of his son caused every nerve in Daniel's body to react.

Daniel held his son like he was holding on for dear life.   He held his child tight, wanting to assure himself that Blade was real; that this moment was real.

Blade needed to touch his daddy; needed to know the man that made him possible.   He'd wanted this touch. . . this very hug only for all of his life.   He felt his own warm tears flow unabashedly, and he didn't care.   He felt the back of his shirt dampen with his father's tears and he *did* care.   He cared that his father cared; he cared that his father held him as tightly as he was holding his father.

Chapter 32

"Sheila, Parker, Frisco, and Sienna . . ." Blade counted off the names of his four siblings, then assured Daniel he would get in touch with each one.

"I'm going to make it my business to see every one of them within the next year, Dad. It's pretty short notice, but I'm going to see if we can all get together sometime during the holiday".

Daniel heard the title, and with the sound of the word 'dad' uttered by his first born, he struggled with all his might to keep the tears behind his eyeballs. While his four younger children referred to him as 'dad', he still wasn't sure that he was deserving of that title from Blade. As Blade chattered away about his plans to meet his four siblings, Daniel looked west toward the setting sun. Although his eyes squinted in response to the piercing late afternoon rays, he held his focus on the bright orange and yellow orb. He inhaled and exhaled slowly, basking in a sense of peace to which he was only now growing accustomed and that he still wasn't yet sure he deserved. He recalled the wisdom Carla had offered so succinctly: "*. . .we can't rewrite the past. . .*".

Daniel suspected that as an officer in the United States Army, Blade must have some fairly important professional obligations. As a young man embarking on his second decade of life and his first real taste of freedom, he expected that Blade would be about the business of cultivating a social life, above everything else. Between his burgeoning social and professional lives, Daniel expected that his son's primary focus would be something other than siblings he had never seen. And yet, he sat in awe as Blade perched himself on the cold concrete steps of his parents porch and chattered happily about the prospect of meeting his four younger siblings. Daniel couldn't help but compare his son's level of maturity with his own at that age. In the face of the blessing he had received in a son of Blade's caliber, Daniel spoke silently to a power greater than himself. Daniel heard his son's enthusiasm about being his son and about being connected to the other children he had sired, and he realized at once just how blessed he was. He came to terms with the notion that despite his years of selfishness, judgment and arrogance, he had been given the greatest gifts possible---the gift of his own flesh being happy to be his flesh; of this child that he had neglected and snubbed, having done so well with his life and yet wanting his daddy to be an active part of his life.

Try as he might to listen to Blade's well laid out plan to be the big brother to his two younger brothers and two sisters, Daniel found himself simply mesmerized by an experience unlike any he had ever had in his entire forty-three years of life . . .an experience of love despite himself; an experience of knowing he was forgiven; an experience of knowing he was truly accepted for who he was, not what someone else wanted or expected him to be.

As he occasionally peeked at the son who favored his father far more than even he, himself, did, Daniel smiled and pinched himself to be certain this was real.

"Could all this goodness be mine?" he asked silently.

"Could I, the one who shunned this very child, be deserving of Blade's time . . . of his attention. . . of his good will?"

Every time his mind raced back to his own misdeeds, Daniel would be, once again, reminded of Carla's words. He decided, in that moment, that those words would become his mantra. He couldn't change the past; he couldn't rewrite history, but he decided that he could and would certainly change his future. "No . . ." he said to himself as he soaked in the warm October sun,". . . I'm not going to charge into either of their lives like some superhero coming to reclaim my place as a father . . . but I will be available to embrace them on whatever terms they will have me".

As he perched on the glider that needed a coat of paint, he looked over at Blade, who was sitting on the step and Daniel smiled. He knew he would remember this day.

And with that, Daniel embraced the peace that had been granted him by a source mightier than any he would ever know.

Chapter 33

"Thanks for keeping an eye on things over there, Daniel. I don't know how I would have managed staying on top of things here and monitoring the contractors there. You're a life saver, big brother".

"Hey. . . not a problem at all" Daniel assured. "Everything looks good over here. The contractors have done an incredible job. This place looks awesome!"

"I'm glad you were able to give this project the last two months it needed, or we would be in trouble for our holidays. I'd promised Creighton a special Christmas this year" Patience shared.

". . . so I'll get to meet the young fellow, at last" Daniel smiled.

"Yep. Mr. Creighton Bright. You know we're in the legal process of changing his name, right?" Patience asked.

"No. I didn't know that . . ." Daniel admitted, leaving the option out there for his sister to share the details of this decision, and she did.

"Yep. He's not a Bright and neither am I. So, we're both going to officially be Milledges come one January" Patience said excitedly.

"Congratulations!" Daniel offered.

"So, other than watching over the renovation . . . and again, I can't thank you enough! . . ." Patience said, ". . . what have you been doing with yourself since you are officially not in the workforce any more?"

". . . officially preparing myself to get right back into it, it seems. Honestly, Patience, I've enjoyed the last few months of doing nothing. Although I was fighting it tooth and nail, I'm glad I went with the retirement, after all. I start school in earnest come three January, so I'm basking in solitude for now. Plus little projects around here have been keeping me busy . . . and, you know what?" Daniel asked without wanting or expecting an answer, " . . . I've been going out to the Mabry place each day . . . you know, I never realized how therapeutic it is to be doing that manual labor out in the fields".

"What?! . . . you in the fields? . . . and what do farmers do this late in the year anyway?" Patience inquired.

"Well, we're doing some underbrush clearing on some of the acreage and pulling collards in the other fields. It's dirty work, but I come home at night feeling good . . . tired, but good. There's something wholesome about being out there" Daniel declared.

"Well, do wonders ever cease?" Patience quipped sarcastically. "My brother, Farmer Francis . . ." she laughed.

"Well, me and Creighton will be getting in on the twenty-second, so make space on your calendar, Mr. Green Acres, for us to go Christmas tree hunting" Patience said.

"Aye, aye, sir . . . oops, I mean, ma'am!" Daniel teased in turn.

Daniel looked around the spacious rooms with their sky high ceilings and shook his head in awe of his sister's foresight.

"What an incredibly smart and thoughtful woman she is" he said out loud in the empty house. Even with upwards of four years before her target retirement, Patience had taken the bold step of settling herself in Bristol Creek. She had purchased what was little more than a lean-to and transformed it into a palatial living space, while at the same time preserving precious elements of her mother's history as part of the structure. Daniel found it ironic that he had never, as a child, seen the house in which his mother had spent her childhood, even though the structure stood less than thirty-minutes from their own home. The old abandoned shack was actually about three quarters of a mile from the Mabry farm. So, all along when he was sneaking out to the country to see Carla, he thought, he was closer to his mother's homestead than he could have imagined.

Patience had secured the old beaten down house and cleared the heirs' rights and now owned the eleven acres free and clear. She kept the original structure and made it the foyer for the new house she constructed. She also took re-usable elements, such as doors, from the original house and incorporated these into the new home. Daniel shook his head in amazement of such a vision. Since his retirement just after Aunt Mary's funeral he had come back to Bristol Creek and oversaw the conclusion of the construction project.

And now Patience and Creighton's home was ready for occupancy just in time for the holidays. They were next door neighbors (meaning at least three quarters of a mile away) to Carla, with whom Patience had become fast friends.

Daniel was pleased that Patience had decided to make Bristol Creek her retirement home. This had been a factor in his own decision to return to his place of birth after retirement. With his children in several states---North Carolina, Arkansas, and Colorado---he couldn't be sure where he, himself, would finally end up, but for now he was comfortable in his childhood home.

Daniel looked forward to spending the holidays with his sister and relished the opportunity to help her put on a traditional Christmas for her teenage son. He was assured also that Blade would be coming to Bristol Creek for the holidays, too.

Daniel and Creighton busied themselves with righting the huge leaning Douglass Fir, as Patience fussed over non electrical decorations in between barking orders at the two men about the steadiness of the eight foot tree.

Daniel exhaled heavily from his nose, with sweat beading over his entire scalp. Creighton, too, slumped his shoulders in an exasperated fashion. The two had invested more than six hours in finding, cutting, and dragging the monstrosity into the house. Now they were expending what seemed like inordinate amounts of energies trying to get the oversized tree to simply stand up straight.

"You know, Creighton, I'm getting tired of your mama ordering us around like we're two of her little privates" Daniel argued in jest.

" . . . and why can't we have lights on the tree, Ma?" Creighton whined.

"No lights?!" Daniel asked in jaw dropping surprise.

"We're going to have an old fashion Christmas, sweetie. . ." Patience assured, ". . . and it will be beautiful. . . with our tree adorned with candy canes and ornaments that we've collected over the years".

". . . no lights. . .?!" Daniel still couldn't imagine a Christmas tree without lights.

"Daniel why don't you bring some of your ornaments to put on our tree?" Patience invited.

"Ornaments . . .?! I ain't got no ornaments!" Daniel fairly barked. "I'm wondering how come we're not gonna' put any lights on this tree?" Daniel continued in his lament.

"You'll see. . ." Patience reiterated, ". . . It'll be just like in the olden days".

Daniel's rolling eyes met his nephew's rolling eyes as the two men continued on their quest to steady the tree. He looked up at the tree that seemed like it ended in the clouds and shook his head in doubt.

"You sure you got enough ornaments to cover this whole tree?" Daniel asked skeptically.

"I do . . .but don't worry. Everybody who comes to Christmas Eve dinner will bring an ornament" Patience assured.

"All of America's gonna' have to come to have enough ornaments to cover this big tree, Ma", Creighton whined some more.

Patience stroked her son's shoulders in assurance.

"It's going to be fine, Creighton".

She then turned her attention to her brother.

"I've got the Cornish hens you wanted, Daniel. Do you need me to do anything with them?"

"No. Thanks for ordering them, though. I'll take care of the cooking. I've got my spices in the car and I'll get those little birds to marinating tonight. They'll be good and flavored by tomorrow afternoon . . .perfect for a slow grill" Daniel smiled.

Patience had spent most of the rest of December 23rd wrapping gifts, and when Daniel arrived on Christmas Eve the house looked and smelled festive. Looking around he was taken to a place of comfort and hominess. Patience had decorated every inch of the house with some kind of holiday garnish, and the huge tree had scented the entire house with the wintery aroma of conifer. It smelled like Christmas and to Daniel it felt like Christmas, too. He couldn't remember being in the holiday spirit like this in a long time. He smiled, as this had been the first time in many, many years that he was in a festive mood. This was the first time in many, many years that he would be part of a family holiday celebration.

The intimate gathering of Patience, Creighton, Daniel, Old Man Mabry and Carla was comfortable, but in Daniel's estimation, the scant few people seemed inadequate for the festive table Patience had set. He was pretty certain that six people could never devour all the food they had prepared. Daniel was well aware that Blade would be coming too and he suspected that he might very well be bringing a guest. Daniel knew also that Patience had invited Aunt Sarah, Aunt Eva, and Uncle Jessie and his wife. She had not gotten RSVP confirmations from either of them, but Daniel reminded her that that didn't mean they weren't coming.

"Listen, girl . . ." he had joked with his sister, ". . . we ain't the kind of people that know noth'in about rsvp'ing".

By nightfall the doorbell was ringing every few minutes as guests arrived. Patience had deliberately scheduled dinner early so people could, if they wished, have time to still make their religious obligations. Plus, she had confessed that she didn't want to be up until all hours of the night, herself. She was still quite the morning person, and would like to have dispensed with most of the guest early in the evening.

Daniel heard the loud rumbling from the living room as he brought in more hens from the patio grill. Eager to see who had arrived this time, he parked his large cookie sheet of tender roasted hen halves on the endless granite kitchen counter and made a mad dash for the great room.

When he turned the corner his eyes just about popped out of their sockets. He couldn't believe what he was seeing or hearing. The high screech and squeals of teenage girls giggling and bantering threw him for a loop.

"Daddy!" He heard the sounds of two adolescent voices, and all of a sudden those sounds that would, at one time, have been a source of annoyance, were, on this night, music to his ears. Before he could begin to orient himself to what was happening around him, four skinny arms were wrapped tightly around his neck and he was inundated with the smells of bubblegum scented perfume and lip gloss--- the very smells and sounds he missed more than anything in his life. He held his two daughters in his arms like there was no tomorrow, and they both showered their father with bubble gum flavored kisses all over his face and head.

At about this time, Frisco peered from around his oldest brother's long legs like he was playing peek-a-boo. He smiled his shy, but mischievous smile with a front tooth still missing. His still-pudgy baby face swelled with joy at seeing his daddy.

"Come her boy!" Daniel said running to his youngest with both glee and tears of joy in his eyes. He wrapped his thick arms around the seven year old and twirled him around like he was still an infant. He eventually got around to taking his eldest into a hug of gratitude. By this time the house was abuzz with all kinds of teenage activity. It would easily be another hour before the family could settle down to the business of eating.

Old Man Mabry asked the blessing with a deeply heart felt prayer that was so much more than the traditional grace. While the adults sat at the formal dining room table, the teenagers took the big table in the huge breakfast nook. Based on all the banter that could be heard from them, Daniel was assured they were all getting along fine and getting to know one another. Blade went back and forth between the two groups. When he took a seat at the adult table, Daniel thanked him profusely.

"Son, you must have been traveling all over the United States of America to make this happen" Uncle Jessie commended.

"Thanks to Sgt. Major Auntie, here . . ." Blade said pointing to Patience. Everyone in the room smiled at Blade's affectionate reference to Patience.

Through the large picture window Daniel noticed the reflection of headlights as a vehicle climbed the slight incline of Patience's driveway. While no one else at the table gave any indication that they saw the high beams from the approaching automobile, Daniel knew that Blade had seen it. He saw Blade look at his watch just as the lights flickered past. Daniel couldn't imagine who else would be coming, but then assumed this must be some guest of Blade's. Before the doorbell rang, Blade was up on his feet and headed in the direction of the monstrously large and heavy door.

"Dad its for you" Blade said.

Even hearing his son say 'dad', it took Daniel a few seconds to respond; he still wasn't entirely accustomed to being called that by Blade. In fact he felt a little shy about being called dad by Blade, especially in the presence of Old Man Mabry and Carla. Before he could react to Blade's summons, John Mabry granted him permission to embrace the honor of Blade's title in his own special way.

"Son, I b'lieve yo boy is call'in you", the old man said with the warmth of a twinkle in his eyes and a broad smile on his face.

Daniel woke himself out of his stupor and sprung the few steps to the foyer and then towards the door. On his way it dawned on him that he wouldn't know anybody in Bristol Creek who would come to visit him, and especially at Patience's new house. He'd only been back in town about six weeks himself, and nobody knew he would be way out in the country with Bristol Creek's newest residents.

By the time he got to the door Blade had stepped back against the foyer wall, but his left hand still rested on the door knob. When Daniel got to the door the glass storm door swung outward and there, before him, stood his prodigal son. He was so happy to see Parker he couldn't think about fighting the tears that had been at the precipice of his eyes for all that evening. All he could do was swaddle his son in his arms and let the emotions he'd been holding back flow out in plump drops of salty tears. Daniel hadn't expected to see any of his children except Blade. To have gotten to see any of them was a gift and he knew Blade had to have worked hard to make that happen. When he held Sienna in his arms earlier, he was determined not to ask about Parker . . . and to now hold his son in his arms . . .

This was a merry Christmas.

Acknowledgements

My sincere thanks to all who have supported, not only this effort, but all my publications. Your prayers, your readership and your kind words of encouragement have become the catalyst for my continued growth. I extend a special thank you to my friend, confidante and editor, MSgt. James E. Nealy, (USAF Ret) who has laboriously, but diligently and meticulously pored through pages upon pages of drafts. Thank you, sir, for keeping your sanity and for helping me keep mine. Thank you also for keeping me grounded.

www.ingramcontent.com/pod-product-compliance
Lightning Source LLC
Chambersburg PA
CBHW022037240626
47154CB00007B/2451